I knocked.

No answer.

When I got tired of knocking, and Mae was starting to get a little hysterical, I went downstairs to the desk and came back up with a bellman and a master key. He unlocked the door and left, and Mae and I walked in.

That's how we came to find Roscoe Kane in the tub, a bottle of Scotch, empty, on the floor nearby, arms floating on the surface, his head bobbing up to the top but his nose and eyes still under water, his thin hair spreading out from his head like spider legs.

Mae didn't scream or faint.

She just dropped to her knees and cried.

I think maybe I cried, too.

Heroes aren't supposed to get drunk and drown in the bathtub, you know. But mine had.

Apparently.

Look for these other Tor Books by Max Allan Collins

THE BABY BLUE RIP-OFF
KILL YOUR DARLINGS
NO CURE FOR DEATH

KILL YOUR DARLINGS

MAX ALLAN COLLINS

TOR

A TOM DOHERTY ASSOCIATES BOOK

KILL YOUR DARLINGS

Copyright © 1984 by Max Allan Collins

Reprinted by arrangement with Walker Publishing Co., Inc.

First Tor Edition: February 1988

A TOR Book

Published by Tom Doherty Associates, Inc.
49 West 24th Street
New York, NY 10010

ISBN: 0-812-50161-6
Can. No.: 0-812-50162-4

Printed in the United States of America

0 9 8 7 6 5 4 3 2 1

In memory of a real hero:
Dave Gerrity

AUTHOR'S NOTE

The Bouchercon is an actual event, an annual convention of mystery writers and readers, which has on a few occasions been held in Chicago (among other places); but the Bouchercon portrayed in this book is a nonexistent one, held only in the minds of the author and his readers. The Private Eye Writers of America is a real organization (of which I am in fact a member); however, that organization should not be held responsible for the fictional manner in which it is used here.

In a nod toward verisimilitude, various real people are occasionally mentioned in the pages to follow, all of whom I've seen attending one or more Bouchercons. It is my hope that anyone I've mentioned will not take offense; and anyone I've failed to mention will not feel slighted.

Also, this is not a *roman à clef*; Roscoe Kane, for example, isn't supposed to represent any one specific author. He is—to invoke the standard auctorial copout, which in this case is *not* a cop-out—a composite. So, among others, are G. Roger Donaldson and Gregg Gorman.

The Crime Tour depicted herein was suggested by material in *Big Al's Official Guide to Chicago-ese* by Bill Reilly (Contemporary Books, 1982).

The aspect of this story relating to Dashiell Hammett is grounded in fact. However, mentions of the estate of Hammett (and its executors) in this work of fiction are not meant to refer to, or reflect upon, the actual Hammett estate (and its executors).

M.A.C.

Part One:
THURSDAY

1

HEROES aren't supposed to die.

But heroes, at least real-life "role model" type heroes (as opposed to such mythic figures as Hercules and Davy Crockett), are human beings; and human beings, even the best of 'em, sooner or later, each and every one, wind up dead.

My hero was dead in a bathtub; drowned, apparently. He'd been drinking heavily, earlier that night. He'd been dead drunk when I walked him up to his hotel room. And now he was just dead.

A few hours before, he'd been vocal—embarrassingly vocal—sitting in the cocktail lounge downstairs. We were in Chicago, in the Americana-Congress Hotel, and it was October.

"There hasn't been a goddamn mystery writer worth reading since Dashiell Hammett died," he slurred, at a table of mystery writers. Tomorrow was day one of the Bouchercon, the annual mystery fan convention.

"You're worth reading," I ventured, smiling, trying to keep it light.

Roscoe Kane, the shoulders of his plaid shirt flecked with dandruff, his patched brown sports jacket slung sloppily over the back of his chair, looked at me with disgust lining every wrinkle of his basset-hound face, his rheumy china-blue eyes like nasty lasers. The hoarse voice wanted to be contemptuous, but sad self-pity got in the way: "I used to be."

Across the table from us, Brett Murtz, in faded blue workshirt and jeans, leaned over and gestured, his long curly hair and free-flowing mustache making him look like a hippie Gene Shalit; he had the kind of enthusiasm it took to have driven here from Colorado in a Datsun.

"I'll bet you could still write a hell of a yarn," he said. "You ought to come out with a new Gat Garson!"

A bigger chill couldn't have fallen across the small party of five if somebody had turned on the air conditioning; the rest of us—me, Peter Christian, Tim Culver—were well aware of Roscoe Kane's unfortunate situation, where publishing was concerned.

But Murtz rushed in where angels fear to tread.

"Don't tell me you've got writer's block!" Murtz said, good-naturedly. "I wrote you a fan letter back when I was in high school, and told you I was trying to be a writer, and said I had a book half-written but was stuck—and that I was afraid I had writer's block—remember? And you wrote me back and said . . ."

" 'There ain't no such thing as writer's block, just blockhead writers,' " Kane said, with a mirthless smile.

Murtz's grin went up in one direction, his mustache in a couple of others. "You remembered!"

I smiled and nodded. "He told me the same thing, two years ago."

Kane said to me, "That's the advice I give to any jackass in that situation, Mallory. I need another Scotch."

A pretty brunette barmaid in a short skirt took care of that; Kane didn't seem to notice her, even when

4

she bent over and gave us a view right off the cover of one of Kane's Gat Garson paperbacks.

I was hoping the question about why Kane wasn't publishing anything—why he hadn't published a new novel in the United States in fifteen years, in fact, and anywhere in the world in the last ten—had been forgotten in the wake of Kane's latest Scotch, a long slow joyless sip of which he took, and then got right into the inevitable harangue.

"I was the biggest name in paperbacks," he said, launching into a variant of a speech I had heard half a dozen times before and read as many times in letters from him. "Spillane came along writing his violent junk, and took the paperback world by storm. It was postwar, and the vets wanted some hair on their books' chests, and the Mick, for all his faults, knew that. You don't take a guy who's been in the Battle of the Bulge and give him a book about a guy in a white suit whose gun goes bang and makes a nice clean tidy little hole in the bad guy's black suit. Naw! You have your guy shoot a big unpleasant bloody hole in the bad guy! A hole you could drive a Mack truck through. That's what a reader who's been through the Second World War goddamn well expects. Carnage. And he doesn't expect the sex to be prim and proper, either. He's looking for it hot and horny. . . ."

Kane was wound up, now; this story used to be delivered more articulately, but the Scotch—not just tonight's—had taken away a few too many brain cells for Kane to be in top form. What he was saying was true, of course. In the postwar paperback boom, sexy, violent novels inspired by the success of Mickey Spillane's Mike Hammer series were the backbone of the fledgling industry. But of Spillane's many imitators only one—Roscoe Kane—had given the Mick a run for the money. Even Richard S. Prather and John D. MacDonald were runners-up, compared to Kane. Why?

"Because I was smart enough to use humor. Oh, not that broad campy crap Prather used to dish out—"

Murtz, hearing one of his idols besmirched, interrupted. "I *like* the Shell Scott stories. . . ."

"They were lousy!" Kane ranted. "My humor was subtle. My stuff was Hammett done tongue-in-cheek."

"Low-key," Peter Christian said, eyes intense behind dark-rimmed glasses. "Somehow the humor never gets in the story's way. Wonderful." Pete is a dark-haired, stocky, vaguely disheveled man who happens to be one of the most knowledgeable guys in the mystery business, having coauthored the definitive *Encyclopedia of Mystery and Detective Fiction* a few years back.

Next to him was Tim Culver, who in his tan corduroy sports jacket and wire-rim glasses looked like Woody Allen's older, better-looking brother. I'd never met him before, and he'd seemed quiet, even shy, as the evening began; but a few drinks loosened him up a bit and he occasionally spoke.

Like now.

"I always got a kick out of your stuff," he told Kane, with a soft-voiced intensity. "It's the Hammett understatement done to a turn. The average reader could appreciate it for its surface—a fast-paced story, well told. And a slightly more hip reader would appreciate the put-on."

The folds of Kane's face turned into a hundred smiles. He liked compliments. He liked them from the likes of Pete, who after all was partly responsible for the *Encyclopedia*, which had given Kane the only literary recognition he'd ever received in his long career. Paperbacks didn't get reviewed back when

6

Kane was doing them; they still don't, mostly. But the kudos from Culver meant even more to him, I'm sure, since Culver was considered by many critics to be the best modern writer working in the Hammett tradition.

I was hoping these compliments would forestall the tragic story that, should Kane tell it, would no doubt end the evening. Because once he got into *that*, the party was over.

"Murtz, Murtz," Kane was muttering, looking suspiciously at the hardworking writer whose counterculture background was still apparent, and even today would label him a "longhair" to a conservative eccentric like Roscoe Kane. "What have you written?"

"Some occult-oriented private eye stuff under a pseudonym," Murtz said casually. Kane asked what, specifically, and Murtz told him, and Kane said he'd never read any of 'em. Trying to hide his hurt, Murtz said he'd sent Kane copies, but Kane ignored that—which is probably what he'd done with the copies.

"Anything else?" Kane said.

Murtz shrugged. "I've ghosted some stuff. I wrote some of the Exterminator books." He was referring to that enormously successful—and enormously silly—paperback series about a Vietnam vet who takes on the Mafia single-handedly, and wins. And wins. And wins.

"Garbage!" Kane shouted, with his usual tact. "The guy that writes that tripe wrote me and said he was a fan, and wondered, considering my 'situation,' if I wanted to do some ghosting for him, myself. It was his way of 'paying me back' for 'teaching him,' the condescending twerp. You know what I told him to do?"

He then told us, just as the *zaftig* waitress was bending delivering Kane's latest Scotch; the effect of the expletives I'm deleting was to put a blush on the paperback-worthy view she'd been continually giving us, in a crass attempt to get us to leave a big tip, no doubt. I planned to leave five bucks. So far.

Maybe Kane's tirade would stop here; his mind was wandering tonight. And his eyes had finally wandered to the waitress, albeit in a clinical way; for a writer of sexy novels, Kane seemed for the most part uninterested.

But Murtz said, "What do you mean, 'your situation'?"

Kane stood. The bar wasn't crowded, but there were people there. Some of them were mystery writers and knew Kane. Some were civilians. All of them were invited to Kane's curtain speech.

"I," he said, in his hoarse, commanding baritone, "was blacklisted! Me. The tenth mostly widely translated author in the world. Me. The best-selling writer of paperback originals in history. Forty million paperbacks. That's just America, kiddies. Forty goddamn million! And they cheated me from word go. They did their own accounting. And I sued them. Sued them! For a million dollars. Melvin Belli, God bless him, got every cent and court costs, and I did something every writer in America *dreams* of . . . I beat the system! I beat the publisher! I won. I won. I won."

He stood and waited, as if expecting applause. Appalled is more like it. Pete Christian was trying to think of something to say, and poor Tim Culver was obviously wishing he were on another planet. Kane sat back down and the bar-room murmur and clink of glasses returned mercifully quickly.

"Only I lost," he admitted. "No publisher in America would touch me. I wrote five Gat Garsons that were never published in the United States. They were published overseas. . . ."

"Yes," Murtz said, nodding, all of this news to him (not the million-dollar lawsuit, which was famous, among writers at least: but the blacklisting of Roscoe Kane). "I have those, in British editions. I always wondered why . . ."

"They're published in sixty-five countries, young man," Kane snapped, "but not here. Not in my own hometown, the old U.S. of A. Not a single one of my books is in print. Nobody wants me here, ain't it funny? The blacklisting bastards!"

"That's nuts!" Murtz said. "No publisher is stupid enough to turn down a sure thing! Even if you did take your publisher for a million, some other publisher would've *grabbed* the Gat Garson series."

"So one would think," Kane said, hoisting his Scotch.

Murtz, though a professional writer and a good one, was thinking like a fan: later, he'd probably, on reflection, figure it out. The heyday of Roscoe Kane was 1950 through 1960. Even then, his phenomenal sales figures had begun to show a downward slant. By the early '60s, and the James Bond spy boom, Kane was out of step; he was still turning out his tough, tongue-in-cheek private eye stories, with no discernible difference between his 1965 style and his 1950. It was in '66 that he went to court, charging the publishers with doctoring the ledgers to deny him his rightful royalties, and the million-dollar lawsuit took several years, during which time Kane did no writing.

By 1970, when he began approaching new publishers with his Gat Garson series, he was sadly out of step, out of date. He had never written a novel that wasn't a Gat Garson story, and as unique and genuine as his talent was, it was a narrow talent, apparently suited only for the sort of tough detective story he'd begun turning out in the 1940s, when he broke in by writing for the renowned pulp magazine, *Black Mask*.

Had Kane not alienated himself from the publishing world by airing its dirty laundry in public, had he not a reputation for (literally) punching editors in the mouth (he broke a hapless copy editor's arm for inserting too many commas into one of his leanly written manuscripts), had he been a normal, non-wavemaking, sane writer, he—and Gat Garson—might have found a new home in the publishing world. His sales figures alone would've been impressive enough to get him a contract with some smaller company looking for a name, even if that name belonged to a guy who made derbies in a world that was wearing sweatbands.

But if Roscoe Kane had been a normal, sane writer, he wouldn't have been Roscoe Kane; he wouldn't have had the stuff to create a figure like Gat Garson, who had spawned twenty-five novels, a radio show, a couple of bad movies and an equally bad TV show, but who (Gat, we're talking about) was a genuine popular culture figure that most folks on the street would even now recognize by name. In Europe, Gat was as well known as Lemmy Caution, and the general European taste for private eyes kept Roscoe Kane in print and even in vogue.

Kane's continuing success in Europe—and his dwindling million—had kept him alive. He was on his third wife now (and his tenth Scotch tonight), and was a cantankerous self-pitying old bastard whose private eye books I read as a kid had made me want to write mysteries when I grew up, and so he was my hero. Still.

And he was standing again.

"The sons of bitches blacklisted me!" he shouted, waving his hands, though not spilling his drink—a trick few of even the most serious drinkers can pull off. "Let's drink a toast to 'em!"

A hushed pall overtook the bar, like the room was one great big cake that fell, and we were the unlucky ingredients. We were all caught in his grip. Lunatics have that power, you know. Any time they want the floor, they can have it; sometimes they use a gun, but more often just obnoxious behavior.

Because there is something irresistible about a lunatic in full swing; somebody out of control who can control all those about him.

"Let's drink a toast to 'em!" He held his glass high. "Let's toast the American publishing industry! The sons of bitches who keep me off the paperback racks!"

He stood there with drink held high, and everybody in the place knew that he would stand there like that till hell froze over or they toasted with him. Some time passed, and it got chillier. But eventually we all toasted with him, and the poor old bastard sat down. The party was over.

"I think I better get some shuteye," he said softly, with a weary, suddenly lucid expression that people sometimes get shortly after behaving like lunatics, realizing what they've just done.

"I'll walk up with you," I said.

"Thanks, kid," he said.

The other men at the table rose and gave him the respectful and friendly goodnights he would've deserved if he hadn't gone over the edge the way he had; these men, like me, loved this sad old guy, and he could've hung naked from the ceiling shooting rubberbands at barmaids and we would've found a way to ignore it, or at least forgive it.

I guided him by the arm—it felt bony, the flesh on it slack. Was this small, shrunken man the guy who'd posed, à la Spillane, in a muscle shirt, wearing a .38, on the back cover of his paperbacks? Sadly, it was. A long, long time ago. We got on an elevator. A wealthy-looking couple stared at Kane disgustedly and I gave 'em back my best withering glance. And I've got a pretty good withering glance to give, when I've a mind to.

We were on Kane's floor, the seventh, and were heading down the corridor to 714, when he said, "I didn't mean what I said."

"You'll have to be more specific, Mr. Kane," I said. "You said a lot of things tonight."

"There you go with that 'Mr. Kane' crap again! I've known you for ten years, Mallory. We 'changed probably a hundred letters. You were to my place half a dozen times. And always 'Mr. Kane.' I hate that!"

But he didn't hate it.

We were at his room.

"What I didn't mean was that thing about no mystery writers since Hammett being worth reading," he said. "Chandler's worth reading."

That was generous of him.

"Do you have your room key, Mr. Kane?"

"In my pocket," he said, getting it. "The Mick's worth reading, too, but don't tell 'im I said so. And John D. And Culver's good."

"Yes."

"And me. I'm still worth reading."

"I know you are."

"And so are you, kid. You are, too."

I smiled, and felt some ambiguous emotion stir in me; I wrote mystery novels myself, in no small part because I had dreamed of being as good as this man one day. I certainly didn't deserve being listed in the exalted company Roscoe had mentioned; and Roscoe knew it—he was just being nice, or as nice as that cantankerous old bastard was capable of being.

Still, hearing him say that felt like getting an A from your favorite teacher—even if your favorite teacher did happen to be dead drunk.

"Thanks, Mr. Kane."

"G'night, kid."

That was the last time I saw him alive.

2

I was on my way back down to the bar, to see if I could drink enough to lose the sad taste in my mouth, when the elevator doors slid open on the fourth floor and Tom Sardini, wearing an off-white shirt and dark slacks and a preoccupied expression, climbed aboard the otherwise empty cubicle. As usual, youthful, handsome Tom (handsome in a baby-face way he tried unsuccessfully to mask with a beard, the mustache of which never seemed wholly grown in) had a glazed look behind his black-rimmed glasses, as if even now he was working on his latest story.

Which he probably was. Sardini, at thirty years of age, was the current Fastest Typewriter in the East, turning out crime novels and westerns and an occasional spy novel (under various pseudonyms), as well as his "top of the line" books about private eye/ex-boxer Jacob Miles (under his own name), at an alarming rate. He worked so fast and wrote so much that writer friends of his told him to slow down, pretending (to themselves as well as Tom) to be worried about his health, while envying his productivity. Tom, meanwhile, sat at his typewriter in his Brooklyn home, writing, collecting royalty checks, quietly turning into a corporation.

"Okay, then," I said, "*don't* speak."

"Mal?" he asked, brightening. "I didn't recognize you!"

"I don't mean to be a pest or anything. You probably got a book to write between here and the ground floor."

He grinned and I grinned and we shook hands.

"It's been a long time," he said.

"It was another Bouchercon in Chicago, as I recall," I said. "Many moons ago."

"You had longer hair then, and a mustache."

I gestured toward his own ever-scraggly mustache/beard and writerly unruly hair. "I looked around and noticed that all the old men had long hair and facial whiskers, and the kids were wearing short, punky hair."

"So you got a haircut. What else is there to do in Port City, Iowa?"

The elevator doors slid open and we walked toward the nearby lounge.

"I keep busy," I said. "I know you New Yorkers find it hard to believe a writer can actually get ideas in Iowa."

We walked into the lounge; Pete Christian and Tim Culver were gone, and Brett Murtz had hopped to another table, where he and several people I didn't recognize had cornered William Campbell Gault, giving him an eager, fannish interrogation. Gault, a dignified but unpretentious man in his early seventies, was the author of a number of fine tough-guy mystery stories, though he was also noted for his sports-oriented young-adult novels.

Tom and I found a table, and the same barmaid who'd helped Roscoe Kane stay knee-deep in Scotch took our orders; I was drinking Pabst from bottles, and Tom was, too, since I was paying. The barmaid was trying for another five-buck tip.

"You know," Tom said, picking up on the Iowa motif, "I somehow can't shake the image of you sitting in a cornfield, a scarecrow looking over your shoulder while you perch on a crate writing stories on lined paper with a stubby pencil."

"Did I ever mention I hate New York?"

"Frequently."

"Well, just for the record, I hate New York."

"You do manage to keep stumbling onto murders, in that little hayseed community of yours."

"Give me a break, Tom. It happened twice. And years apart."

"You're just the only mystery writer I know who's done research *that* active. Still live in a trailer?"

"I moved out."

"How come? Did it finally sink into that landfill it was sitting on? Or did selling your books to the TV movie folks make you *nouveau* rich?"

"That's *riche*. I think. As for the trailer, I got tired of being mistaken for Jim Rockford. Anyway, I did come into some dough from those TV sales, and got a chance to pick up a little house."

"On the prairie?"

"No, with a river view."

"Sounds real Mark Twain."

"It's a house, not a houseboat, Tom. I don't want 'em to start mistaking me for Travis McGee."

"Well, you *did* put a color in one of your titles."

"Hey, be fair, Tom—last I heard, the rainbow was in the public domain. You didn't like that book much, did you?"

He shrugged. "I liked the book okay. I just like your short stories better."

I shrugged back. "Can't make a living at that. Books are where it's at. Maybe you'll like the next one; maybe I'll put you in it."

"That'd help," he admitted. "Just promise me you won't make any cracks about my name sounding fishy."

"If you slip me a fin, it's a deal."

His grin under the almost-mustache was infectious. "Very funny. You know, I can't say I was nuts about what the TV folks did to your first book."

I groaned, swigged some beer. "Couldn't we talk about something more pleasant? Like my hernia operation?"

But Tom was enjoying my misery, and plunged on, archly: "Granted, they made some minor changes. They switched the locale from rural Iowa to Los Angeles, and your white-bread hero was played by O. J. Simpson. And they changed the ending, 'cause they didn't think the high school sweetheart ought to be involved in the murder."

"Otherwise it was a faithful rendition," I said.

Now Tom seemed to feel a little bad about needling me, and leaned forward and said, with no archness at all, "Don't forget what James M. Cain said when the reporter asked him what he thought about what the movies had done to his books: 'Nobody did anything to my books,' he said, 'they're right back up there on the shelf, just like I wrote 'em.'"

"O. J. Simpson isn't going to be in the next movie."

"That's good."

"They're talking Scott Baio."

"Maybe we better get some more beers. That better be some house."

"Oh, it is. Got a roof and everything. I bought a new car, too."

"What was wrong with the van?"

17

"Just not my style. I'm not a kid anymore. I turned thirty-three last time I looked."

"What car d'you buy?"

"A silver Firebird."

"No kidding? That's what Rockford drives."

I'd just bought the car a few days ago, and this drive into Chicago, on a cold, rainy October afternoon, had been my first extended experience behind its wheel. I liked the feeling of driving a sporty car, my last two vehicles having been an old Rambler and that van Tom had asked about; but the dreariness of the day, and the realization that I had finally gotten a sporty car at an age, or anyway "time of life," when it didn't mean as much to me, had a sobering effect on me (unlike the Pabst I was now chugging).

I'd been nervous about attending the Bouchercon; the last one of these I'd attended, I was a barely published writer of short stories—now I was a more visible "author" of two published hardcover novels, one of which had just been nominated for Novel of the Year by the Private Eye Writers of America (whose awards ceremonies were traditionally held at Bouchercon). I considered the nomination a fluke—for one thing, the book had gotten (deservedly) mixed reviews; for another, the hero wasn't a private eye and so, technically, the book probably shouldn't have even been in the running. But knowing I didn't deserve to win—knowing I didn't have a prayer to win—didn't keep me from writing an acceptance speech over and over again in my brain on the four-hour drive from Port City to Chicago.

"I understand your idol Roscoe Kane's here," Tom said.

"Yeah, you just missed him."

"Damn it! Will you introduce me tomorrow?"

"Of course."

"I bet meeting him must be an experience."

"It certainly is."

"He's one of my favorites, too, you know."

Tom was one of the world's foremost authorities on private eye fiction, and one of the genre's biggest enthusiasts; getting on his list of favorites didn't make you one of the elite. Even I was on. In fact, the first fan letter I ever had was from Tom. God bless him.

"What do you think about this Hammett thing?" he said.

"What Hammett thing?"

"The new Hammett book."

"What, you mean the latest biography, the one by Cynthia Crystal?"

"No, no . . . I mean the new novel."

I picked up the bottle of Pabst he'd been pouring from and looked it over.

"Tom," I said. "I don't know how to break this to you, but Hammett's been dead since '61, and that's put a crimp in his publishing efforts. Considering he stopped writing around '34, I hardly think there's a new Hammett novel, unless it was written with a Ouija board."

"It's an unpublished book that he wrote in the twenties. A lost manuscript that got found a few months ago."

"Yeah, right, in a box in the back of Murder Ink bookstore next to *MacBeth Meets the Bowery Boys* by Francis Bacon and Huntz Hall."

"Mal, this is for real. The manuscript's been authenticated. The Hammett estate is standing behind the thing."

"Are they involved in the publication? Will they hold the copyright?"

"I believe so."

"Then they stand to gain. Sounds hinky to me."

Tom made a face; this time he looked at my Pabst bottle to check what *I* was drinking. "Hey, the executors of the estate aren't going to hoax the public where Hammett's concerned. If they were out for a buck, they wouldn't 've kept so many of his short stories from being reprinted in book form; they're fussy about what Hammett stuff gets put back in print. But how could they stand in the way of a newly discovered book-length work?"

I was starting to think Tom was telling the truth and not taking advantage of a hick from Iowa who'd been drinking all evening.

"Hammett's my favorite writer," I said. "I'd love to read a new Hammett book. So would a few other people. Don't play games with me, boy. What's the deal?"

The novel, a mystery featuring Hammett's famous Continental Op character, was entitled *The Secret Emperor*, and until recently had been believed left unfinished by Hammett, in its earliest stages, as some notes in the Hammett collection at the University of Texas would indicate. But, apparently, during 1927—a year when Dashiell Hammett had been thought to have temporarily given up writing to go back to the ad copy-writing game—Hammett had revised and completed the manuscript.

"Hammett's editor at *Black Mask*, old Cap Shaw, had encouraged him to do this book," Tom said, "but when Hammett showed it to him, the Captain was disappointed."

"Why? Was it bad?"

"How should I know? I haven't read it yet; damn few people have. But Shaw is said to've been disappointed because Hammett didn't construct it as a serial, so that Shaw could run it in installments in *Black Mask*."

"Which is how Hammett's first book, *Red Harvest*, and most of his other books were put together," I said.

"Right. This one was all of a piece. Hammett apparently lost confidence in the book, and never showed it to a major publisher; instead, he sold first rights to a little California firm that specialized in rental library hardbacks—westerns and detective stories. Why that company never printed the book is, you should pardon the expression, a mystery. But here's the rub: they never really folded, that house. They were swallowed up by several other publishing firms, the latest of which is Mystery House."

"Mystery House! That's Gregg Gorman's company."

"You know Gorman?"

"I know the s.o.b."

"Sounds like a warm relationship."

"That's another story. Keep going with yours."

"Well as you know, Gorman's a specialist in reprinting 'important' mystery fiction . . . stuff the hardcore mystery fans are willing to buy, in rather expensive editions. You collect that stuff?"

"Some of it," I admitted. "I bought *The Complete Race Williams* by Carroll John Daly, in a slipcased set."

Daly's character Race Williams was, historically, fiction's first hard-boiled private eye; but Daly was a rotten if energetic writer—"Okay, rats . . . make a move and I'll open you up, and see what you had for supper!"—and only a fool (like me) would buy the complete Race Williams novels in a slipcased set. I said so to Tom.

"Well, meet another fool. Apparently there were around twenty-five hundred of us that foolish, and at two-hundred dollars a boxed set, that ain't hay. And it's just one of many editions Gorman's brought out."

I nodded, sourly. "Gorman's done some good work, for scholars and mystery-fan fools like us. But he's still an s.o.b."

"So I gather. Anyway, Gorman uncovered this manuscript, somehow, and rather than publish it himself, sent it out for bid to all the major publishers last month. He worked out some kind of deal with the Hammett estate—since all he owned was first publication rights—and everybody seems to be happy."

This was an important literary event, to say the least; Hammett was, by nearly universal acclamation, the finest mystery writer America has yet produced (or is ever likely to). One of a handful of American crime writers (with Chandler and possibly James M. Cain) to achieve a reputation of literary worth transcending the genre, Hammett published a mere five novels: *Red Harvest*, a violent shoot-'em-up that paved the way for the Spillane school; *The Dain Curse*, a complex story about a family with skeletons in its closet that set the pattern for Chandler and Ross Macdonald; *The Maltese Falcon*, the most famous private eye story of all, starring the most famous private eye of all, Sam Spade; *The Glass Key*, the understated crime story that was Hammett's personal favorite (and Roscoe Kane's favorite Hammett, incidentally); and *The Thin Man*, which combined the tough mystery with the comedy of manners, and gave the world (particularly Hollywood) Nick and Nora Charles and their terrier, Asta.

And now a posthumous work: *The Secret Emperor*.

"Who's bringing it out?"

"Random House."

"What did they pay?"

"Six figures, is what I hear. What six, exactly, I couldn't say."

"Here's to capitalism," I said, clinking my glass of

beer to Tom's. Considering Hammett's leftist politics, I made sure my facetiousness was self-evident, in case his ghost was nearby; and if Hammett's ghost was anywhere, it would be in a bar.

"For a Hammett fan you don't seem too thrilled at the prospect of reading a 'new' Op novel."

"I just don't trust Gorman," I said.

"I understand the book is authentic."

"First-rate Hammett?"

"What I heard was 'authentic' Hammett. It's actually his first novel, so it's bound to be a lesser work."

"Not really. He'd been writing short stories for a good many years by '27. If it isn't close to *Red Harvest* in tone and quality, I . . . I don't know."

Tom was amused. "Suspect fraud, Mal?"

"I smell Gregg Gorman, is all."

A pretty woman in her early forties, wearing a Sam Spade trenchcoat, her hands thrust in its pockets, was in the doorway, looking anxiously around the bar room. I knew her: Mae Kane, Roscoe's current—and in my estimation best—wife. She had wide Joan Crawford eyes. An out-of-date silver pageboy hairdo that had been Kane's idea swung in twin arcs as she looked about the room. Irritation tugged at the red slash of her mouth.

Then she saw me, and the slash turned into a nice smile, an attractive smile, and she moved toward our table.

Tom and I stood.

Mae came over and hugged me. I hugged her back and looked at her and saw a face like that of a Hollywood beauty who was aging but doing it well. In fact, Mae had been an actress, once, a stage actress and then a radio and TV personality of some national prominence, of the Faye Emerson variety—until her first husband (a banker, now deceased) had turned her into a housewife—a housewife with a maid and furs, admittedly, but a housewife. She and Roscoe had met four years ago on a talk show she was doing for a local TV station, in Milwaukee, where they both were living; after her banker husband's fatal coronary, Mae had gotten back into broadcasting in a small way. Meanwhile, Roscoe swept her off her feet. I'd spent a weekend with them a year ago and, after three years, they still behaved like newlyweds. She was the bright glow in the midst of Roscoe's currently dark universe; the glow that made that universe worth existing in, despite Roscoe's publishing "situation."

I introduced Tom and Mae, and Tom said some gushy but sincere things about Roscoe Kane and Gat Garson.

Mae seemed to have other things on her mind.

"Something's wrong," she said. "I was supposed to meet Roscoe in the lobby, at eleven. It's almost midnight."

"Didn't you come down together?"

"No. I had some work to do at the station, and Roscoe wanted to come here a day early, to do some sort of business or other. He took a plane down yesterday; I drove down this evening."

I gestured for Mae to sit and she reluctantly did. "Nothing to worry about," I said. "Roscoe just got a little wound up tonight. . . ."

"Wound up as in 'tight'?" she asked; her eyes looked sad.

"Yeah. He must've forgot he was supposed to meet you. He went up to his room half an hour ago."

She glanced at Tom, wondering if she should get into this with a stranger present; then she said, "He's been drinking too much, Mal."

"He always has as long as I've known him."

24

"Not like this. Did he tell you about the fire?"

"What fire?"

"He drank himself to sleep a few weeks ago. Nothing unusual about that. But I was at work, at the station. He was smoking . . . he's supposed to have given that up, doctor's orders, but when I'm not around to hound him, he'll have a smoke. He fell asleep with the cigarette in his hand, it dropped to the floor and burned up half the carpet, and if the neighbor hadn't been walking her dog and seen smoke, the house—not to mention Roscoe—would've been incinerated."

I didn't know what to say; I just tried to look sympathetic and shocked and concerned, which was no trick, because I was all of those things. But I just didn't know what you could do to keep a sad proud chronic drinker, whose career was a shambles, from drinking. I wasn't sure I wanted to. I wasn't sure Roscoe should have that taken away from him. What else did he have?

"I thought I was enough," Mae said. She had a blank expression, but you could almost see her heart breaking in the watery shimmer of her eyes. "We were so in love. We still are. But we had plans to get his career going again. We had more than just plans. He was writing again. Only these past few months, he's been drinking more than writing."

Tom raised his eyebrows in a sideways glance that Mae wasn't supposed to see; but she did, and picked up on how uncomfortable Tom was hearing all this, and she seemed suddenly embarrassed.

She stood. "Well. Maybe I should just take a room of my own."

"Whatever for?" I asked.

"Roscoe said he planned to register under a phony name. He likes to mingle with people, with fans, but on his own terms; doesn't like to have them dropping by his hotel room at all hours. But he went off and neglected to tell me what name he'd be using. The clerk is the night clerk and wasn't on duty when my husband checked in, so describing him won't get me a key or a room number."

"I know his room number. It's 714. You want me to take you up there?"

She smiled; she really looked lovely. She had the right kind of lines in her face—she was in her forties like Faye Dunaway is in her forties. I felt a little surge of sexual interest in her, which immediately made me feel guilty.

I said, "I'd love to walk you up to your room . . . your husband's room."

She picked up on my nervous slip and her one-sided, wry smile showed she liked compliments as much as her husband.

"Nice meeting you, Mr. Sardini," she said to Tom, shaking his hand, nodding to him as he half-rose a little clumsily, surprised by the attention. "Excuse my little soap opera theatrics," she said. "I used to be in show business, you know." As if that explained it. Which it probably did.

Tom said something polite and I told him to order me another Pabst, I'd be back soon.

We picked up her bags from the bellman in the Congress' fancy front lobby; I carried them. In the elevator, Mae said, "Did Roscoe tell you about his new publishing deal?"

"No," I said, surprised he had one. And more surprised that, if so, he hadn't mentioned it tonight, when he was filibustering on publishers.

"Well, he does. Not much of a deal. A small publishing house wants to do the five Gat Garsons that have never been published in the United States. A man named Gorman is responsible."

26

Him again.

"Gorman's done some important work," I said, "in getting undeservedly neglected mysteries back in print." The s.o.b.

"Roscoe was excited about it for a while," she said, a little puzzled. "But his euphoria was short-lived. It seemed, after the first rush, to depress him even more. It was a little after that that he started really drinking heavily again."

The elevator doors slid open on seven; the Congress was an old hotel, and, despite frequent remodelings, looked it. We wound around several halls to 714.

I knocked.

No answer.

When I got tired of knocking, and Mae was starting to get a little hysterical, I went downstairs to the desk and came back up with a bellman and a master key. He unlocked the door and left, and Mae and I walked in.

That's how we came to find Roscoe Kane in the tub, a bottle of Scotch, empty, on the floor nearby, Roscoe himself slumped in the nearly full tub, his arms floating on the surface, his head bobbing up to the top but his nose and eyes still under water, his thin hair spreading out from his head like spider legs.

Mae didn't scream or faint.

She just dropped to her knees and cried.

I think maybe I cried, too.

Heroes aren't supposed to get drunk and drown in the bathtub, you know. But mine had.

Apparently.

3

WHEN Mae got up off her knees, she became more than a little unglued; she wanted me to help her haul Roscoe Kane out of the bathtub and onto one of the beds, but I made her leave him where he was. She got a little angry.

"You heartless son of a bitch!" she said. "How can you . . . leave him there like that! You bastard!"

And I held on to her arms, loosely, so she could pound small hard fists into my chest. It hurt a bit, but she seemed to need to do it. And the pain distracted me, which was nice. The physical pain, I mean; it got my attention, pushing the emotional pain momentarily away.

Then she looked at my face—she told me later she saw tears streaked there and it made her sorry for pummeling me—and she was in my arms, crying, body heaving with sobs, holding on to me, holding on for dear life.

"We have to leave him as he is," I said, finally, quietly. "We can't touch anything."

She drew back from me, her eyes wide, a look of sudden, sharp curiosity giving her that Joan Crawford '40s movie star presence again.

"Why?" That came out in three or four breathy syllables; it was an accusation and a question and a threat, all at once.

"Look, Mae. Mr. Kane . . . Roscoe . . . he's dead. It isn't going to hurt him any to stay put."

"You bastard." Softly; knowing I was right, but not liking it, or me, at the moment.

"Roscoe didn't die of natural causes, Mae. He drowned. An accidental death, probably, but one that's going to require some care and caution. We have to call the desk, now, and get the manager up here."

She sighed, nodded, and the theatrics—which I think were not false theatrics, but quite genuine theatrics, if that makes any sense to you, the affected melodrama that becomes real if a person makes enough of a habit of it—sort of drained out of her and she sat in her coat on the edge of one of the room's two double beds with her shoulders slumped; and she looked old. She kept her back to the open doorway to the bathroom.

The manager came up within minutes—well, actually, the assistant manager, or *an* assistant manager. I never quite got that straight. But I did manage to gather he'd only had this position of responsibility a few weeks. He was younger than me, and dark, and had an Indian accent and a blazer with a hotel crest; he was immaculately groomed and very polite, like Andy Kaufman doing his foreign-man routine.

He was also a little thrown by all this.

"I have never had a dead guest in my hotel before," he said. As if Roscoe Kane had checked in that way.

"Well, you've got one now. Don't you think you should call the police and get somebody from the coroner's office over here?"

"It's very late."

29

"The cops are open twenty-four hours. Somebody'll come."

"If a guest dies of natural causes, we're to phone a certain funeral home. It is written on my calendar."

"That's nice; that way you'll know what day it is when your guests drop dead."

He gave me a look that said my humor eluded him; it eluded me, actually. I was lapsing into talking like Gat Garson, I suddenly realized. I felt embarrassed.

"Look," I said, "a drowning is not a natural death." We were standing just outside the bathroom where Roscoe still bathed. Mae was on the far double bed, sitting, staring at a draped window. She didn't seem to be listening, but I kept my voice down just the same. "And," I added, "I think this may be something other than just an accidental drowning."

The brown eyes in the brown face were so alert it was uncomfortable meeting them. The earnestness there was disconcerting.

Very softly, I said, "This may be murder."

Without asking for an explanation, he said, "I'll call the police."

I touched his arm, stopping him, as he was already on the move.

"Just tell them we need somebody from the coroner's office," I whispered. "Don't say murder. That's premature."

He nodded curtly and went to the phone.

A heavyset man in a brown baggy suit arrived in forty-five minutes; I'd had room service bring up some gin and Mae was pretty much sedated by now, and lying on the turned-down bed in her coat, not asleep, but not awake. I'd offered her my room, so she wouldn't have to share the suite with her late husband, still soaking in the tub, but she wouldn't

30

hear it. She wouldn't let me turn on the radio or TV, either. The gin she was agreeable to.

The man from the coroner's office with his brown baggy suit and his brown baggy eyes and his brown bag took a look at the scene and without asking a question said, "Drowned in the tub, eh." He was alone in the bathroom, the assistant manager and I standing just outside listening as his voice echoed in there. He gestured at the bottle on the floor without picking it up. "Drank himself to a stupor, drowned in the tub."

And he walked out of the bathroom and said, "Who are you?"

I gave him my name and said I was a friend of the deceased, and that I'd found the body in the presence of the deceased's wife. The man from the coroner's office glanced over at her and an expression that tried to be world-weary betrayed his cynicism. When he said, "I don't want to bother her with questions," it came more out of wanting to get out of here quickly than compassion for the widow.

He said, "Did the deceased drink heavily?"

"Yes. I spent most of the evening with him, and he drank heavily, yes."

"I mean, did he drink heavily in general?"

I told him yes, and repeated the story about the near tragedy with the burning cigarette that Mae had recounted to me earlier.

The man from the coroner's office nodded and said, "Well, why don't you let the hotel man, here, call the funeral home and get that poor guy out of the tub."

"Are you going to take any pictures?" I asked.

He looked at me like I'd asked him to dance.

"What the hell for," he said. Not a question; just some words strung together that weren't looking for an answer, and in fact he pushed by me and went over to be by himself and started filling out some

31

official papers on a clipboard from his brown doctor bag.

"Didn't you notice anything funny in that bathroom?" I asked him.

"Oh sure. Lot of laughs in there."

"The floor's bone dry."

"So? He drowned by passing out in the tub; he wouldn't have been splashing around."

"There's only one towel hanging in that bathroom."

"So?"

"Normally, there'd be at least two; I'm in a single room and there were four towels provided."

He thought that over.

I went on: "If somebody had held him down in that tub, and drowned him, there would've been lots of splashing around. And a very wet floor that would need mopping up."

"And leaving sopping wet towels behind would've been a dead giveaway, so the murderer ditched them."

"Could be."

"Hey, pal. I ain't Quincy. This guy passed out in the tub, okay?" He went back to his form-filling. But as he did, he asked the assistant manager, who'd been patiently listening to all this, "Do you see anything in the lack of towels?"

The assistant manager said, "Sometimes we run short of clean towels. If the guest sleeps in and keeps a do-not-disturb sign on his door—the maid may be short of towels by the time she gets around to doing the room. Perhaps leaving only one. Particularly if a guest, like Mr. Kane, is the room's sole occupant. Such things happen in a hotel."

The man from the coroner's office looked up from his paperwork and his expression said, "See?"

I turned to the assistant manager. "Is there a closet around here, with a laundry hamper?"

That seemed a ridiculous question to him, but politeness was his way, so he said, "Most certainly."

"Where?"

"Just across and down several doors."

I went out, by myself, and found a numberless door ajar just down the hall and opened it and found a closet with a big hamper with three wet, sopped towels on the top. I didn't touch anything; just went quickly back.

The man from the coroner's office came with me reluctantly, sighing the way only a big man sighs, and examined the sopping towels, with his hands.

"Watch it!" I said. "Should you be touching those?"

He looked at me like I was a four-year-old. A stupid one. "Yeah, right, these wet towels pick up the prints of killers like an X ray. Why don't you give this a rest, and me a break?"

He walked back across the hall to room 714 and I followed him in, not knowing whether to feel angry or idiotic. I settled for a little of both.

"You're not calling the police in, then," I said.

"No." An unfriendly smile and a shake of the head.

"This could be a murder."

"This is an accident. You're giving me a real major pain in the ass, pal. What's your part in this, anyway?"

"I found the body."

"Yeah, yeah. Who are you? Just a friend of the family?"

"Yeah."

"Well, go sit with the wife. Be supportive. Leave me do my job."

"Sir. I think you may be blowing this." I couldn't quite get indignant; I wasn't sure I was right.

"I know my job. Leave me do my job. What do you do for a living, pal, that makes you such an expert?"

Great.

"I'm a writer," I said.

"What, a reporter?"

"Mystery writer," I mumbled.

"What?"

"Mystery writer."

He gave me a big-city smile that said I was the most pathetic thing he'd seen all day, in a day full of seeing pathetic things and feeling superior to all of them.

Part of me wanted to punch him, but part of me also thought maybe his attitude was right on target. My hero had drunk himself senseless and drowned in the tub. Maybe I ought to grow up and accept that sorry fact.

I took one more try.

"Listen," I said. "I used to be a cop. Please don't write me off as a kook. Hear me out."

"Why, you got something new to say?"

"Come with me."

I walked him into the bathroom; Roscoe hadn't moved.

"That empty bottle of Scotch," I said, pointing to it. "I was with Mr. Kane until maybe forty minutes before his wife and I found the body. And you're saying during that time he supposedly drank this whole bottle of Scotch and passed out and drowned? I just don't believe it. And where's the glass? Roscoe Kane didn't drink out of a bottle."

"You brought me in here for this twaddle? A drunk who doesn't drink out of a bottle? You think forty minutes isn't time enough to drink some Scotch and drown and die?"

"A *whole bottle*?"

"Who says it was a full bottle? He had it in his room and 'd been nursing it all day, probably; he just killed it here in the tub. And it killed him."

I didn't have anything to counter that with. I found myself looking at Roscoe, nude, old, skinny, dead. I looked at him through a watery haze, not all of it in the tub.

The man from the coroner's office put a hand on my shoulder; it was a gesture that was meant to be conciliatory, but it was too firm a hand, the impatience in the man getting the best of him. I shook it off.

He raised his two hands in a gesture that sought a truce, and then pointed toward Roscoe Kane. "Come look at something," he said.

I went closer to the tub; looked where the fat stubby finger was pointing.

"Do you see any bruises?" he said. "Look at his shoulders, where he'd have likely been held down. Take a close look."

I did.

"No bruises," he said.

"Suppose he *had* passed out or fell asleep in the tub or something, but with his head up out of the water—and somebody held him under; even if he woke up during that, it'd be over fairly quick."

"Sure, but he'd be bruised."

"Not necessarily. He's skinny. Frail. It wouldn't take much to hold him under and. . ."

"Listen—what was your name? Mallory?—you could be right. One in a hundred is about your odds. But there's just not enough to go on. He has a history of drinking; a past, recent accident where he drank himself to sleep and almost died because of it. The evidence here indicates no struggle; it, in point of fact, indicates he passed out and died. Now. Let it go."

Suddenly I felt he was right; I felt embarrassed. I nodded, said, "Yeah, yeah. You're probably right. Sorry."

35

"It's okay."

That was when the ambulance guys from the funeral home arrived with a stretcher and a body bag. I helped them dry Roscoe Kane off before they put him in and zipped him up and wheeled him out. I told them we'd call tomorrow and give them the particulars.

So Roscoe Kane was gone, and soon so was the man from the coroner's office. Mae was asleep. Fitfully so, but asleep.

I thought about sleeping on the other bed, so she wouldn't be alone when she woke up; but decided just to leave a note, with my room number, if she wanted me and my help. I was, at this point, intruding.

So I got out of there.

Back in my room, in bed, I kept going over the scene of the . . . crime? Accident? I couldn't make up my mind.

Roscoe Kane had never attended a Bouchercon, or any fan gathering before, for that matter; and I was the one who'd convinced him to come to this one. Me. I brought him here. All but put him in that damn tub. Tom, who was the current president of the Private Eye Writers of America, had asked me to get Kane to the 'con, so that the PWA could surprise him with their annual Life Achievement Award.

"We're a young organization," Tom had told me over the phone a few months back, "and we need the sort of publicity we can stir up by having a Roscoe Kane on hand. Kane may not be a household word these days, but a man who sold that many books—but who has *never* been honored for his work, in fact who has been pilloried for it—will make good fodder for the media. We can get ink, we can get on the tube, we can build some recognition for our group, and some credibility. I need you to make sure Kane is there in person, Mal . . . otherwise we're dead in the water."

I'd made sure Kane was here, all right. Dead in the water.

The last thought I remember having, before drifting off to sleep, was, "Where the hell's Gat Garson when you really need him?"

Part Two:
FRIDAY

4

THE phone rang and scared hell out of me.

I'd been sleeping deeply, and was in the midst of a disturbing, just-short-of-delirious dream in which Gat Garson and I were chasing Roscoe Kane's killer down the corridors of the Hotel Caligari; a faceless killer whose form shifted but who had a gun, and Garson said, "Look out!" as the killer fired the gun at me and the phone-ring came out the barrel. My eyes jumped open and saw the phone, and I stopped it before it could ring again. I spoke thickly into the receiver: "Mae?"

It wasn't Mae Kane; it was the wake-up call I'd left for ten o'clock, figuring I'd wake before that. But I hadn't. I thanked the operator, hung up, sat and rubbed my eyes with the heels of my hands. The feel of the dream was still with me, a physical sensation, a film in my mind as real as my morning mouth. I stumbled up out of bed and brushed my teeth, and my mouth tasted better, but the dream was still there.

And so was the death of Roscoe Kane; that wasn't something I could shake easily, either.

I drew a bath.

I went to the window and looked out at Michigan Avenue; the park was across there, but you could barely see it. Fog had settled on Chicago like a private eye's porkpie hat. It would've struck me as nice, appropriate weather for a Bouchercon; only, fun-and-games murder à la mystery books and movies seemed, after last night, trivial, in bad taste.

I got in the hot tub. A lot of people prefer taking showers these days, particularly in hotels; but writers—like Roscoe Kane and I—like to take baths. We can sit and soak and ruminate, or maybe read; a bath is passive, and lets you do that. Showers are entirely too active for my taste. It's tough to read in a shower.

But I wasn't reading, I was ruminating. Thinking about Roscoe sitting in the tub last night, a floor above me, sitting and soaking and drinking and passing out and dying. Had he done that? Had he really done that?

I washed up and got the hell out of the tub.

I sat naked on the edge of the bed and called down to the desk to see if there'd been any messages from Mae; there hadn't been. Perhaps she was still sleeping. I could check later.

I threw on a sweater and jeans and went down to the lobby. The coffee shop was called the Gazebo and was an affair full of latticework and lawn chairs and fake foliage. The convention didn't begin officially till late this afternoon, but most of the mystery writer guests were already here, so the booths and tables in the restaurant were filled with familiar faces. William Campbell Gault and his wife were having a leisurely late breakfast at one table; at another, Tim Culver and Cynthia Crystal were finishing up theirs. Cynthia, a lovely Grace Kelly blonde in her midthirties, had won the Mystery Writers of America Edgar award last year for *The Children Are Hiding*. Mystery-magazine columnist and short-story master R. Edward

Porter was having coffee with Bill DeAngelo in a side booth.

DeAngelo was a big, gregarious guy in his early thirties, with the usual beard and Poe-ishly long hair of the younger mystery writer. He was wearing a black suit with a tie but was not quite getting away with it—the suit meant for us to take him as a serious-minded adult, but his good-humored enthusiasm for his work, and for life, was childlike and endearing. DeAngelo had won two Edgars, once for a hardcover mystery novel and again the next year for a paperback; he was a very young man to have pulled that off—I couldn't seem to find a way to resent or dislike him for it, though, try as I might.

He smiled when he saw me, and stuck his hand out to be shaken; I complied.

"I understand we're on another panel together," he said.

We'd been on a panel at the last Bouchercon I'd attended, also in Chicago, years before; I was a little surprised—and flattered—he remembered that, and me.

"Really?" I said. "I haven't seen the program listing yet. But I did tell the 'con organizers I was willing to make a fool out of myself, if they wanted me to."

"I think we're on the catchall panel," he said. "We're supposed to talk about the 'state of the mystery'—that's so general a topic as to be meaningless."

"Is Donaldson on it?"

"The Guest of Honor? No. Disappointed?"

"No."

A wicked little smile formed under the mustache. "Don't you like Donaldson?"

"Never met him."

"I meant his books."

"I know you did. I'm just being evasive."

43

Ed Porter smiled a little. "Care to join us?"

"Thank you, no—I see Sardini and Murtz over there. I have to go talk over some things with Tom."

Porter, a soft-spoken, gentlemanly man in his fifties, said, "Sorry to hear about Roscoe Kane." His concern was genuine, his manner somber.

DeAngelo's cheery look dropped away. "Terrible thing. Hell of a way to start a Bouchercon. It's like a bad joke."

"I wish it were a joke," I said.

"Roscoe was a nice man," Ed said, "and an underrated writer."

I nodded.

DeAngelo said, "I never got to meet the guy, but he was very, very good. I think he was better than Chandler."

That was a controversial thing to say out loud at a Bouchercon, Chandler having achieved a sort of sainthood approaching Sir Arthur Conan Doyle's. I liked DeAngelo for that—even if he had won two Edgars.

I stopped at the table where Tim Culver and Cynthia Crystal were just finishing up what appeared to be a rather silent breakfast. Cynthia smiled briefly on first seeing me, then apparently made the Roscoe Kane connection, because her expression turned sympathetic.

"Mal," she said, rising, holding a hand out to me, which I took. She still had the same trim model's figure, in a stylishly cut gray slacks outfit; she was wearing her pale blond hair short these days.

"Hi, Cynthia," I said.

There was something besides sympathy in her eyes, nervousness, maybe. It was impossible for Cynthia to be anything but graceful, yet somehow this seemed an awkward moment for her. "I'm very, very sorry to hear about Roscoe Kane's death. I know what he meant to you." She let go of my hand; swallowed. "Do sit down for a moment."

Culver, without rising, motioned toward an empty chair—they were two at a table for four—and I sat.

"It's been a long time, Cynthia," I said.

"Since that other Bouchercon, here in Chicago. How many years ago?"

"I've lost track."

"Don't you ever get to New York?"

"Once in a while."

"Call next time."

"I will."

Culver searched for words. "This must be a rough morning for you," he said. "I know Roscoe Kane meant a lot to you."

"Yes, he did. We sort of had the final audience with him, I guess, last night in the bar."

Culver sipped some coffee, sighed heavily. "At least I got to tell the man how much I admired his writing. For all the money he made, he had precious little recognition."

"I would have thought money was his primary goal," Cynthia said, with a little shrug. She turned to me, still sympathetic. "I don't mean to be unkind, Mal. I know Kane was your mentor, of sorts. I just mean, I don't think we should feel too sorry for him, in terms of his writing career. Beyond the publishing problems of his later years, I mean. Because I don't think Roscoe Kane had any literary pretentions; he was a craftsman, if you will, and he made his fortune, and I'd imagine he felt quite content having done so."

Culver shook his head no. "I disagree. Kane wasn't a hack by any means"—he glanced at me—"you must remember that 'craftsman' is Cynthia's euphemism for hack." He looked back at her sharply. "You seem to have forgotten he was a peer of Hammett and

45

Chandler's, the last 'star performer' of the original *Black Mask* crowd. . . ."

Cynthia half-smiled. "Don't you think I know that?" she said, with the gentlest condescension.

Something was going on beneath the surface of this literary discussion that I couldn't quite pick up on; and I wasn't sure I wanted to.

Culver looked at me again. "Anyway, I'm very sorry, Mallory. Just wanted you to know."

"I appreciate that. And I'm sure Roscoe appreciated hearing your words of praise, too. You're one of the few modern mystery writers he had any respect for."

Culver smiled a little. "That's nice to hear."

"I'm glad to meet you, too," I said. "I've always admired your McClain series. And I'm also a big fan of your brother's. Is he attending the convention?"

Culver's face froze.

"No," he said. He plucked the check from the table and stood. "Excuse me while I take care of this," he said, and rose and strode off toward the mini-gazebo housing the cashier.

"What was that all about?" I asked Cynthia.

"He and his brother don't speak," she said. "It's simple envy on both their parts. . . . Tim gets the good reviews, and Curt gets the Hollywood sales."

Culver's twin brother, Curt—who wrote under the name Curt Clark—was the author of numerous comedy caper novels, a good half dozen of which had been snapped up by the movies. But it was Culver's Hammett-like novels about professional thief McClain that had earned the critical raves, as well as a couple of Edgars and several overseas awards.

"Didn't mean to step on any toes," I said.

"Oh, he's just in a gloomy mood today," she said. "I think being with Roscoe Kane so shortly before his death made Tim a little dour, shall we say. Contemplating his own mortality—which of course is the male equivalent of the navel."

She said this with the tiniest cocktail-party smile, and got a genuine smile out of me, despite my own mood. She was able to get away with saying the nastiest things by saying them in the most good-natured, offhand way.

"I liked your Hammett biography," I said. "How'd you swing the cooperation of the estate?"

"Tact and patience," she said. "Something the men who'd approached the estate hadn't bothered trying."

"I have to admit I was surprised you wrote a book about a tough-guy writer, what with your leaning toward the more genteel sort of mystery."

Cynthia had made her reputation writing drawing-room mysteries, intelligent, urbane American versions of the Agatha Christie formula. Lately she'd begun doing occasional "big" books, suspense novels in the vein of Mary Higgins Clark; at this she'd again been critically and commercially successful, and was similarly successful with her Hammett bio.

"I've always admired Hammett," she said. "That's no secret. My own work is sort of an unlikely marriage between Hammett and Christie. But the tough mystery story beyond Hammett gets silly very quickly. Chandler has his merits, I suppose, but who else? Mickey Spillane? Don't spoil my breakfast. Ross Macdonald? Possibly. But how you can take the likes of Roscoe Kane seriously—and I mean no disrespect, I'm talking about the man's work, and nothing else—mystifies me."

The table tension hadn't departed with Culver.

"You're embarrassed to see me again, aren't you?" I said.

She shrugged; the cocktail-party smile settled uneasily on one side of her face. She lit a cigarette and handled it gracefully, almost regally, but underneath it were nerves. Even nervous, though, she seemed somehow calm; a bundle of contradictions, Cynthia Crystal was—cool and warm, bitchy and sweet. Whatever, she was a beautiful woman. I had told her so, once.

"I still have a crush on you," I said.

She laughed. "That's so like you, that word. 'Crush.' Are you destined to be an overgrown adolescent your entire life, Mal? Will you never grow up?"

I shrugged. "Yes and no," I said.

Her smile turned gentle and suddenly her brittle manner fell away.

"Yes, damn it," she admitted, "I *am* embarrassed at seeing you again. The last time I saw you, I treated you badly. I know it. And you know it."

I shook my head no. "You treated me the way I deserved to be treated. I misread the situation, and you put me straight. Let's leave it at that."

She leaned over and gave me a kiss on the cheek.

"Friends?" she said.

I held a hand out and she took it, shook it.

"Friends," I said.

Culver was on his way back to the table, finally having worked his way through the line to pay the check.

"You just like older men, that's all," I said.

"He's a better writer than you, too," she said with a wicked smile, and the sort of natural charm that made a remark like that seem a compliment.

I smirked. "You're just saying that 'cause it's true."

She patted my hand and I rose.

I nodded to Culver as he approached and he at me, and I went on to join Sardini and Murtz in a booth.

"Mal!" Tom said, having been too deep in conversation with Murtz to notice me come in. "Jesus, sit down! You must've been through it last night."

"The news about Roscoe Kane sure got around fast. I didn't tell anybody. Has Mae Kane been down or something?"

Murtz made a disgusted expression under the every-which-way-but-trimmed mustache. "The hotel leaked it, apparently; reporters were around for a couple of hours, starting about eight, questioning every mystery writer they could get a-hold of. I'm surprised they didn't track you down."

"They've talked to Mae, then?"

Tom said, "My understanding is she gave them a brief statement this morning. She mentioned that she'd been with a friend of the family when she found Kane's body, but didn't give 'em your name. I figured it was you, since you went up with her from the bar last night, and I mentioned that to some of our fellow wordsmiths—but not to the reporters. The word spread among the people here—but nobody tipped the reporters off that a mystery writer helped find the body. Nobody said much to the reporters at all, frankly, let alone hand 'em a juicy sidebar like that."

"Why's that?"

Murtz had a cynically amused smile going. "Well, the press sure wasn't here 'cause Kane was a public figure; they vaguely knew who he was, of course. It's more the sick joke novelty of a mystery writer dying at a mystery convention. An oddity, a cute ironic sidelight."

"Who was here?"

Tom said, "A woman and a cameraman from the *Trib*. A guy and a cameraman from the *Sun Times*. Word is some TV people will be around this afternoon, when the 'con officially opens, to do a live minicam thing on the six o'clock news."

The waitress came over at that point, and I had thought I wanted breakfast, but suddenly coffee seemed all my stomach could face.

"Has Mae been down?" I said.

Sardini shook his head no. "She talked to the reporters in her room. Just for a little while."

I was surprised she hadn't called me for some support; she was a strong woman, though, and had plenty of media experience. She could handle herself.

"Tom," I said, "I'm assuming you'd like me to ask her to stick around until the awards ceremony Saturday."

Tom shrugged elaborately, shook his head no, then broke out into a chagrined smile and admitted, "Yes. I don't want to sound like as much of a media ghoul as those reporters, but we were depending on Roscoe—to get us a little ink."

Well, he'd done that much for them already.

"It'd be good if we could get Mrs. Kane to accept the award for her husband," Tom was saying as the waitress refilled our coffee cups. "I feel like a creep saying so, but we can use the publicity that'd bring."

"I don't think you're out of line, Tom," I said. "I want now more than ever to see Roscoe Kane given some public recognition."

"Then you'll talk to Mae Kane?"

"I'll talk to her. Give it my best shot."

"Thanks, Mal. Sorry to even mention it, really. . . ."

"It's okay. I brought it up."

"Uh, would you mind," Murtz ventured, "telling us what really happened last night?"

I told them; I took it easy on my suspicions, but I didn't leave my suspicions out.

And Murtz said, "D'you really think he was murdered, Mal? Or have you just read too many mysteries?"

I tried to smile but it went sour. "I don't know. Maybe I wrote too many. I found a body one other time, and it was murder—clearly murder. Remember? Maybe I've got delusions of being an amateur detective now."

"Maybe you're just researching your next book," Tom offered, then realized that sounded uglier than he'd meant it to, and added, "I didn't mean that exactly that way, Mal. . . ."

"It's okay," I said. "I'm not sure myself, what to do or what to think. All I know is I'm depressed at losing a friend."

Tom smiled tightly. "He was more than a friend. He was your damn idol. Your hero."

I nodded. "You're right. He was my hero. I've always been something of a hero worshipper. When I was a little kid my hero was Peter Pan; I even had a little green outfit I wore around—quote me, Sardini, and your ass is history! Then it was Batman, and I wore a mask and swung around on a rope for a couple of years. And then around junior high, the Saint was my main man . . . first the TV version, then the books. And then I discovered Gat Garson, and you know those pictures of Kane, in muscleman T-shirts, posing with guns and dogs and such on the backs of his books?"

"Yeah," Murtz said. "He was spoofing Spillane doing the same thing."

"I didn't know that at the time," I said. "I discovered Kane and Gat Garson first—Spillane and Mike Hammer came later, for me. My uncle Richard had some

51

Gat Garson paperbacks in his attic, and I found 'em, and my uncle found *me*, looking at them. He only grinned and said, 'Take 'em home with you if you want,' and I did ... under my coat. The pictures of Kane on the back of the books made me transfer my hero worship from Gat Garson to the guy who *thought up* Gat Garson. It was exciting to me, seeing these pictures of a tough-looking writer, who was a *real person*; I could never hope to be Gat Garson—by twelve, I was hip enough to know that—but I could be Roscoe Kane when I grew up, if I worked at it hard enough. And in high school I started trying to write my little stories. Sending 'em out in the mail. Piling up rejections. My detective was called Matt Savage. You probably had a Matt Savage, too, Sardini; you, too, Murtz."

They were smiling, nodding.

"I had about three heroes, in my life. Real-life heroes I looked up to. During my teen idol phase, I liked Bobby Darin—probably 'cause 'Mack the Knife' was a blood-and-guts crime yarn—had pics of him plastered all over the walls of my room ... next to the Elke Sommer pics, that is. She wasn't my hero, but there was a place for her. And I liked Jack Webb. That movie, 'Pete Kelly's Blues,' you guys ever see that? That shootout in the ballroom at the end, the rainstorm outside? Great! I always wanted to write Webb a letter and tell him how much I admired his work, but I wanted to wait until I'd written something I was *really* proud of, a book I could send him, as a fan who made good. Then last Christmas he died. I felt like I'd lost my best friend. I moped around. Everybody thought I was nuts. I took it damn near as hard as when my folks died. Crazy. Darin and Webb and Kane, they weren't my only heroes, of course; I had the usual ones ... John Wayne, Bogie,

JFK. They're all dead. Darin died after open-heart surgery at age thirty-seven, you know. Kane was the last one. The last living one. I'm thirty-three years old and feel old as hell, 'cause all my goddamn heroes are dead."

I pounded the table with my fist; I surprised myself with the force it exerted, coffee cups jumping all around.

Sardini reached across the booth and put a hand on my arm. "Mal. Are you all right?"

"Haven't you ever seen a tough guy cry before? I'll .see you guys later."

I went back up to my room; the maid, a black woman about twenty-three, was in there and said, "You didn't have no sign on the door."

I didn't follow that. I said so.

"You don't want the room made up," she said, defensively, "you gots to leave the do-not-disturb sign on the door."

"That's okay," I said. "Sorry to interrupt—you go on with your work. I'll go for a walk or something."

I was to the elevators when it occurred to me to go back and ask her something.

"Miss?"

She turned and gave me a sullen stare. She said nothing.

"Did you work yesterday?"

"I work damn near every day, mister."

"Please back off a little. I'm not trying to give you a bad time or anything. I just wondered if you worked yesterday, because I wanted to ask you if you'd run short of towels."

"Huh?"

"Let me start over. Do you work just on this floor?"

"No such luxury."

"Did you happen to make up room 714 yesterday afternoon?"

She smirked and pointed upward with a thumb. "Yeah, so what?"

"It was a late make-up, wasn't it? The guest had left the do-not-disturb sign on his door till late afternoon, right?"

Unimpressed, bored, she nodded. "I gots work to do, mister."

"Were you short on towels?"

"No, I wasn't short on towels."

"You weren't. How many towels did you leave in 714?"

"You're crazy, man. I gots work to do."

I showed her a five.

"How many towels?"

She snatched the bill out of my hand.

"Four," she snapped. "How many you think?"

5

THERE was a do-not-disturb sign on the knob of door 714.

Hardly surprising, considering what Mae Kane had been through; but an unpleasant little ironic reminder of why I was here. . . .

I knocked, and when there was no answer, knocked again, then paused to say, "Mae? It's me—Mal."

A few seconds later the door opened a ways and Mae's face appeared over the taut nightlatch chain, a game little smile in the midst of the pretty but puffy face.

"Hello, Mal," she said. "You're a dear, but . . I'm not really up to visitors right now. . . ."

"Sure," I said. "I understand. But we need to talk, soon as you're up to it. It's important we talk."

The big brown long-lashed eyes, which had a red filigree this morning, narrowed and the lipstick-free lips pursed; she nodded and let me in.

Her bags were packed, by the door.

"When are you leaving?" I asked her.

She went over to the far bed and sat down, crossing pretty, nyloned legs; though she wore no make-up, she was a stunningly beautiful woman: her high-necked dress, brown and silky, clung to her trim figure, and her hair was its wig-perfect twin arcs of silver.

Her sexual attractiveness had always bothered me when her husband was alive, constantly made me feel ashamed of the impulses she stirred; now that he was dead, the guilt was like a heavy coat I was required to wear, perhaps because the zipper was caught.

"I'll be driving back to Milwaukee this afternoon," she said finally. Her voice was husky; it was always husky, but it was especially husky today. Alcohol husky; grief husky.

I sat on the edge of the other bed and faced her. "I really don't mean to be a bother," I said.

She managed a sad little one-sided smile. "You're no bother," she said. "I don't know what I'd 've done without you there last night. I came completely apart."

"I wasn't the epitome of cool myself. I suppose you need to get right home, to make arrangements and everything."

She shook her head. "I made all the arrangements by phone, this morning. A local funeral home is driving Roscoe back this afternoon to a funeral home in Milwaukee. There'll be a little service Monday afternoon. Roscoe didn't have many friends, you know. Some reporters, some people in a writer's club he had helped out. A few blue-collar drinking buddies. Just a handful."

"I'll be there."

"Drive all the way to Milwaukee just for that? It's a sweet thought, Mal, but Roscoe would tell you to save your gas."

I smiled. "He would at that. But I'll still be there. Have you contacted Evelyn?"

Her face turned into a cold, stony mask.

"I tried," she said. "She wasn't home."

Evelyn was Roscoe's second wife; she lived in Milwaukee, too. There was much bad blood between Mae and Evelyn, though why Mae was so bitter when, to be frank, it was she who stole Roscoe away from Evelyn, I couldn't say. I did know, from personal experience, that Evelyn and Roscoe had built a marriage on combat: Evelyn, like Roscoe, was a heavy drinker, and they had battled verbally almost constantly, occasionally getting physical, their hostility erupting in mutual slap-'n'-slug fests. It hadn't been an idyllic marriage, by any means.

"I *did* get through to Jerome," she said. "He took it hard. I was surprised, actually; he and his father had hardly seen each other in recent years."

Jerome Kane was Roscoe's only child, though he wasn't a child any longer, but a man in his forties whose profession—fashion designer—had embarrassed his macho old man. Roscoe had never come to grips with his son's homosexuality, either, and would deny it if it came up in conversation. "Just because the kid designs dresses," Roscoe would say, "that doesn't make him a fruit salad—that's a bigger cliche' than Gat Garson!" (As a matter of fact, some critics in *The Armchair Detective* and other mystery fanzines had built a case for Gat Garson being a latent homosexual; to my knowledge, Roscoe never saw those articles—he didn't follow the fan magazines, and I certainly would never show such articles to him.)

"Will Jerome be flying in for the funeral?" I asked. I felt awkward referring to Roscoe Kane's son by his first name, since I'd never met him.

"Actually, he's already here," Mae said.

"What? I thought he lived in San Francisco—"

"He does, but he's visiting friends in Chicago, coincidentally. Apparently he and his father had dinner together last night."

"That's funny. Roscoe never mentioned it. And when I ran into him in the lobby last night, he'd just gotten back from dinner, he said."

"You would think Roscoe'd have mentioned it, wouldn't you? Well, Jerome mentioned it to me, right off. In fact, he said he and his father had gotten along 'famously.' Their best meeting in years."

"I hope Jerome isn't exaggerating. It'd be nice to think Roscoe and his son came to terms with each other, after all these years."

Mae's smile was almost wistful. "Yes, it would. I'd like to think Roscoe had some happy moments on his last day. His last months have been ... well ... stormy."

"What was bugging him?"

"I don't know. I really don't know. You'd think with Gorman planning to publish the Gat Garsons, it would've given him a shot in the arm. But I can't say it did."

"Getting back to Jerome," I said. "He's staying over for the funeral, I take it."

"Yes."

"I'd like to meet him."

"I can give you the number where he is staying."

"That'd be nice. Thank you."

There was a brief, awkward silence, which Mae broke after a few moments: "I talked to some reporters this morning."

"I heard you did."

"I was surprised they'd be interested in my husband. I thought Roscoe was ... well, sort of a has-been. Is it cruel of me to say so?"

"Not really," I said. "Realistic, maybe. Not cruel. I'm afraid . . . and I don't mean to be cruel by pointing this out . . . but I'm afraid the media folks are just picking up on the fact that a once-famous mystery writer died a somewhat mysterious death on the eve of a mystery convention."

She nodded, her smile a bitter line. "I'm afraid you're right. I sensed that, from the tenor of their questions. I didn't give them your name, for that very reason. I thought if they found out another mystery writer had discovered Roscoe's body, they'd make something out of it."

"I quite agree with you."

"I haven't seen any of the papers yet. . . ."

"Too early."

"Well . . . do you think they'll say anything about— how was it you put it?—the somewhat 'mysterious' nature of Roscoe's death?"

I shrugged.

"I certainly hope not," she said. "This is unpleasant enough without that sort of exploitation creeping in. As an old media maven myself, I can just see them stooping to that. Ugh."

That made it harder for me to say what I'd come here to say.

"Mae," I said.

"Yes?"

"I said I needed to talk to you."

"You implied it was urgent, as a matter of fact. Is there something you're having trouble getting to? Something you're having trouble saying?" She smiled, and there was no bitterness in it, but plenty of sex appeal, damn it. "That isn't like you, Mallory. You usually have plenty to say."

"Yeah"—I grinned—"I am a little long-winded sometimes. I had a critic give me hell for that once."

"I remember Roscoe mentioning that . . . in one of his periodic diatribes against critics in general. As I recall, one reviewer called you 'verbose,' and another 'curt,' for the same piece of work. So what does that make you?"

I shrugged, smiled. "Curtly verbose?"

"Perhaps." She smiled. "Mal."

"Yes?"

"Get to the point."

"Yes. Mae. I think there really *may* be something . . . 'mysterious' about Roscoe's death. I think he may have been murdered."

She leaned forward; her dark eyes flared, then narrowed, boring into me.

"Explain," she said curtly.

I explained, verbosely. I went through what I had told the assistant coroner; she'd been in the room while I did that, but she'd been gin-sedated, so this was all new to her. As I spoke, she reached for her purse on the nightstand and got some cigarettes out, tapped one down on the cigarette pack (Lucky Strikes, like Roscoe and Gat Garson smoked—not a very ladylike cigarette, but she made smoking them a sensuous affair) and lit up, listening intently. When I got to the part about the maid remembering delivering four towels to 714, her eyes got Joan Crawford–wide again.

"My God," she said. "I believe he *was* murdered."

And she reached for the phone. Almost lurched for it.

I put my hand on hers, stopping her; her hand was warm, and I drew mine away. I hated myself for the attraction I felt for her. She was old enough to be my mother, almost; she was my hero's widow of less than a day.

"I thought that through already," I said. "I even called the police, got the name of the assistant coroner from last night—which is Myers, incidentally—and was ready to make the call, when it occurred to me how little I had."

With a trembling urgency in her voice, she said, "You can prove the point you were trying to make last night, about the towels! That's a *lot!*"

I shook my head no. "It's very little. It's hardly anything. Oh, it'd be enough for Gat Garson. But I don't think the Chicago coroner's office is going to give a damn."

"Why?"

"Who's to say that maid's story's going to hold up? Why should she remember servicing a specific room, a day later? Will she be so damn sure of herself on a witness stand, at an inquest, as she was when she was looking at my five-dollar bill? Even if she's believed, how do you build a murder investigation on some wet towels being tossed in a hamper? Who's to say Roscoe didn't bathe that afternoon, before going out for dinner with his son? In which case, he'd have gotten several towels wet; perhaps he himself took the wet towels with him, looking for a closet to get some fresh ones. And when he found the closet, he didn't find any clean towels, but the hamper was right there and so he dumped the wet ones in. Or perhaps another maid came in late in the day and turned down the beds—they *were* turned down, remember?—and got rid of the wet towels, but didn't have any fresh ones to leave, so . . . anyway, it would be a fine piece of evidence in a mystery novel. But at a coroner's inquest, it would be shrugged off twelve ways to Tuesday."

Her face was damn near as pale as her hair. Her eyes were wet. A tear trickled out of one them, making a shiny trail on her cheek. Her fists were clenched and so was her jaw, which was trembling.

I said, "I'd like to do something about this. My instinct is Roscoe was murdered. Or at least, may have been. But we don't have enough to go to the police with."

"I think you should. I think you should call Mr. Myers and tell him what you found out."

"All right, I will. But nothing will come of it."

She stabbed the cigarette out in a glass Americana-Congress ashtray on the nightstand. "Damn it, if Roscoe was murdered, we can't just let it *lay* there! We've got to *do* something, Mal!"

"I know. I know."

We sat and looked at each other; she leaned forward, got a crinkly smile going and stroked my face, in what she probably thought was a motherly fashion. Her skirt was hiked up over her knees, and I wanted to throw myself on her—or out a window.

"Poor Mal," she said. "Poor, poor Mal."

"Poor Roscoe," I said. "I feel fine."

"Do you? Do you really?"

And her mask of composure slipped and she was crying into her cupped hands.

I stood, hoping how I felt about her didn't show.

"I shouldn't have told you," I said. "I should've let it ride."

"You can't let murder ride," she said, sobbing.

"That's a Gat Garson line," I said.

"I know," she said. "Chapter One, *Kiss or Kill.*"

"You were Roscoe's fan, too, weren't you?"

"He was my hero," she said.

I touched her shoulder. Like a son, I hoped.

I said, "Let me poke around a little. Ask some questions. I'll keep my suspicions to myself. I don't want the media to get hold of this, not yet, anyway."

"All right—" She sniffed.

"And I wanted to ask you a big favor. Stick around till tomorrow."

She cocked her head, looking at me close. "Oh? Why?"

"There's a presentation tomorrow afternoon, by the Private Eye Writers of America. They were going to give Roscoe their Life Achievement Award; now that it's going to be posthumous, well . . . they'd like you to be there to accept it."

She smiled bravely. "I'd like that very much."

"It *will* attract some media attention, I've got to warn you."

"This sounds like the right kind of media attention."

"I agree. Enough of that kind of media attention might get Roscoe Kane's books back into print, where they belong."

"That would be nice. I'll be proud to stay, to accept Roscoe's award."

"Thanks. Besides, if I *am* going to ask some questions around, about Roscoe, I'd like you available, so I can check back with you . . . you know, compare notes."

"That's probably a good idea."

"It would be, if I knew where to start."

"Well, nothing was stolen from the room," she said. "There was five hundred dollars in Roscoe's suitcase—cash. Plus credit cards and his watch, which was expensive. Some other things."

"Your point being?"

She had taken a tissue from her purse and was dabbing her red eyes. "It wasn't robbery. It wasn't somebody looting a hotel room who happened upon somebody bathing in the room or something."

"Right. It had to be somebody Roscoe knew. Somebody he knew well enough to be able to let approach him in the tub before he bothered getting up and out."

"Not necessarily," she said. "He could've been sleeping in the tub, when whoever it was came in. Or he could've passed out, like the coroner's man said—only with his head against the edge or back of the tub, not in the water."

"True. But how did 'whoever-it-was' get in?"

"With a key from the desk, maybe? Why don't you ask down there. Hotels can be pretty careless, sometimes, about handing out keys."

"Good thought. Of course, your husband may simply have left the door unlocked, or even ajar. Particularly if he was expecting somebody."

"Yes, but, *who?*"

"Was there anyone staying in the hotel Roscoe knew?"

"Some of the mystery writers. Gorman, of course."

"Gorman's here? In the hotel? He lives in a Chicago suburb; why would he stay overnight in the hotel?"

She shrugged. "I suppose because it's easier to just stay here, throughout the convention, then drive back and forth. He has a dealer's table, I understand."

There was a book dealers' room, where rare and current books would be for sale throughout the Bouchercon.

"How well do you know Gorman?" I asked.

She grimaced. "Too well. Obnoxious man. I do know Roscoe had business to discuss here with him."

"I think I better look that s.o.b. up."

"Oh, you've met Gregg Gorman, then? He *is* a charmer."

"Only if you're a snake."

"Mal, promise me you'll call that assistant coroner. Myers. Tell him you've spoken with me, and that I take this quite seriously. Perhaps that will do some good."

"Perhaps. Can you think of anyone else who might've had a grudge against your husband, who's in the hotel, or in Chicago at all?"

"No," she said. "But if you're right about the towels . . . *somebody* had a hell of a grudge against him."

"Maybe I can find that somebody."

"I hope to hell you can," she said.

She got up and hugged me, gave me a motherly kiss on the mouth, smiled at me.

"I look a mess, don't I?" she said.

"You look terrific. You always look terrific."

"You like me, don't you, Mal?"

"Of course I like you."

"Why don't you come see me in Milwaukee sometime? In a few months. When we're both . . . feeling a little better."

"I don't think so, Mae."

"Bad taste of me to mention that, hmm, Mal? No respect for my dead husband? Let me tell you something. I loved Roscoe very much. But our relationship . . . hadn't been physical for a long time. I wouldn't like the world to know that—to know that macho Roscoe Kane couldn't get it up for his lovely bride— but I don't think he'd mind you knowing."

"I think he would," I said, feeling creepy suddenly.

"Maybe," she admitted; she was still very close to me. Her breath was on my face, and there was still some gin in it; I could forgive her for this, because of what she'd been through, and the gin, but I couldn't forgive myself for what I felt.

She continued: "You're like Roscoe. You're like the young Roscoe I never met. You . . . you made him very happy, in his last years, Mal. You paid him the sort of . . . literary respect he never thought to get.

When everybody else had forgotten him, you came to him like Milwaukee was Mecca and he was a guru." She should've said Mohammed, but she wasn't a writer, so she could get away with imprecise metaphors. "You were like a son to him. He never thought much of his faggot boy, Jerome ... harsh to say it that way, but Roscoe dearly loved to hate homosexuals. And he and his son could never be close, not the way you and Roscoe were close."

The tears were back in her eyes; slowly, they began streaming down her cheeks.

"You, Mal," she said. "You're the young Roscoe Kane, in a way. The Roscoe I never got to know. Not in the ... Biblical sense, anyway. ..." The wicked little smile, in the midst of the tears, was incongruous, and very, very sexy. "The son he never had, the husband I never quite had. ..."

"Please, Mae ..."

"Mal. Come see me sometime. That's more Mae West, than Mae Kane, isn't it? Well, take it any way you like. In a few months, I'll need to be close to somebody. And I'd like to be close to Roscoe, but he's gone. Even impotent, he was more of a man than any other man I ever knew. Come see me ... it's the closest I can come to being close to Roscoe again. Could you do that for me?"

"Maybe," I said. Not ever. No way; despite how much I wanted to.

"And find out what happened to my husband, will you?"

"I'll try."

"If anyone can, it's you," she said.

"What we need is Gat Garson."

"I'll settle for Mallory."

I touched her wet face and found my way out.

66

6

"BOUCHERCON, Chicago-Style" was the official title of this year's 'con, though the nickname "Crime City Capers" had appeared on the advance flyers. Chicago, the "fabulous clipjoint" as mystery writer Fredric Brown had dubbed it, was the perfect setting for a mystery convention: the place where the Outfit was born and John Dillinger died, site of the St. Valentine's Day Massacre, home of the Untouchables, setting for the Gat Garson tales. A fitting spot for mystery writers, critics, publishers and fans to gather, and discuss crime and punishment, fantasy-style.

Bouchercon was founded in 1970, in honor of *New York Times* critic Anthony Boucher, who had died in 1968—actually, "Boucher" was a pseudonym of Anthony Parker White. White was an author of science fiction, and classical, puzzle-style whodunits of the sort Cynthia Crystal was inclined toward, and which interested me about as much as lace doilies and Gilbert and Sullivan revivals. But Boucher was a well-respected critic, and had done perhaps as much as anyone to legitimize mystery fiction, and his was a fine name to grace this annual mystery convention.

The convention rotated annually from a city on the West Coast, to an eastern city, to a midwestern city.

The state of my finances had thus far kept me from attending any but those in the Midwest, and I'd missed the last one of those, in Milwaukee, blowing my chance to meet Mickey Spillane, whose appearance had by all accounts been a show stopper. Spillane, like Roscoe Kane, had rarely had a kind word said about him critically, and, despite his massive man-on-the-street popularity, hard-core mystery fandom hadn't treated the Mick well, either, as one crowd rallied around the Agatha Christie puzzle school, and the other around Hammett and Chandler, the tough-but-literary mystery school, of which Spillane was thought to be a bastard offspring. Since Kane was thought to be a bastard offspring of Spillane, you can guess how the critics treated Gat Garson—when they treated him at all.

It would've been nice to have seen Spillane honored at a Bouchercon, since Anthony Boucher's *New York Times* reviews had been among the most brutal of the many anti-Spillane critiques. Seeing Roscoe Kane—and Gat Garson—being honored at this year's Bouchercon, receiving the Life Achievement Award from the Private Eye Writers of America, no less, would have been a sweet sort of justice, since Boucher had trashed Kane and Gat Garson in a manner that made his Spillane reviews seem complimentary.

Boucher was an astute critic, but he was wrong about Spillane (and came to admit it, in his later reviews) and he was wrong about Roscoe Kane (though that he never admitted). With Roscoe dead, the honors would still come, and probably would be more effusive, as posthumous honors tend to be; but there would be a hollow ring to them. Honoring the dead is so easy. And so pointless.

Or is it? At least a writer, even a paperback writer like Roscoe Kane, gets a grab at the brass ring of immortality. You never know; something you write just might last ... assuming that all of us, including our books, aren't turned to radioactive dust any second now, of course. Short of that, the writer, any writer, even the popular-fiction writer like Roscoe Kane—following the tradition of such popular-fiction writers as Shakespeare, Dickens and Dostoevsky, crime writers all—has an honest (if long) shot at living on through his words.

On the other hand, royalty checks made out to the author's estate are not this author's idea of a good time.

"Is this a private conversation or can anybody join in?"

I looked up.

She was small—petite, even—and her straight, shoulder-length hair was the dark brown you mistake for black if the light isn't hitting it just right. Her eyes were the same color.

"Was I talking to myself?" I said, embarrassed. I was sitting alone in a booth in the Artistic Café, just up Michigan Avenue from the Congress; I'd wanted to get away from the hotel and the Bouchercon guests, and from past experience I remembered the Artistic, in the Fine Arts Building, where young actresses and ballerinas, in tights and leg-warmers and other form-fitting artsy-type duds, often wandered in for coffee. The Artistic was a good place for me to sit and think, and if thinking got old, be distracted by young actresses and ballerinas in tights.

"You were moving your lips," she said, sitting down. She had a pixie face, pert, cute; she'd have made a great hippie, ten or fifteen years earlier.

"Was I making any audible sounds?" I asked.

"Just a sort of murmur," she said, her lips doing a wry little dance around the words as they came out.

But she wasn't a dancer, or an actress, at least not one here to use one of the Fine Arts Building studios. She had on a *Noir* sweatshirt—black deco letters barely visible on dark blue— and her designer jeans were snug (not that there's any other kind). *Noir* was a mystery fanzine I had subscribed to a while back, because somebody had told me the editor'd been reviewing my books favorably; that sounded like my kind of reading, so I sent them a check. So what if Gregg Gorman was the publisher.

Anyway, I figured she was here for Bouchercon, and said, "I figure you must be here for Bouchercon."

"Shrewd deduction," she said; the corners of her mouth went up, and the rest of her mouth was a wavering line, making a terrific wry smile. She had a great mouth, this girl. Whoops, make that "woman": I could tell right off she wouldn't appreciate being referred to as a girl.

"Do I know you?" I said. "Or is that wishful thinking?"

"Do I look familiar?"

"I've seen you before, or somebody who looks a lot like you. Maybe a movie star or something."

"Brother. Hope that isn't dialogue you're trying out for your next story—you usually give that guy in your books better lines."

I managed a grin. "Things I say often seem more clever on the printed page."

"The movie star line won't."

"Maybe you're right. So. You know who I am."

She grinned back at me; she had a thousand smiles, this one, all of them terrific, most of them wry. "Don't be too proud of yourself. It's my job to know who you are."

I snapped my fingers. "Kathy Wickman!"

She nodded; pointed to her *Noir* sweatshirt, giving me a great excuse to take a look at how the word *Noir* rolled with the flow of her. She had the sort of breasts Gat Garson would no doubt describe as "pert, perfect handfuls, straining for their independence"; I, of course, would find a less sexist way to put it, though I can't think of one at the moment.

"It doesn't take *that* long to read the word *Noir*," she said, with a one-sided wry smile. Make that 1001 smiles.

"I flunked Evelyn Wood," I explained; I extended a hand across the table and we shook hands—hers was slim, cool, smooth. Mine was—who cares?

"You may remember, I dropped you a note about your first novel," she said. "I just had to comment, personally, on that chapter about your hero's rites of adolescence."

"That was a nice letter; thanks."

"The letter you wrote back was nice, too. That chapter really hit me; kind of unusual to find it plopped down in the middle of mystery novel."

"That chapter was all true, every word of it," I said. "I couldn't use everything that really happened, actually—some of the things my *real* first love pulled on me outstrip anything the fictionalized one in my book did."

"Really? Say—why don't we get together for dinner, sometime over this Bouchercon weekend? I'd love to hear the stuff that didn't make it into that chapter."

"My outtakes would interest you, huh?" I shook my head. "I don't know if I could be forced to talk about myself like that; I'm really very modest and shy. How about tonight?"

"Okay—" She smiled; this one wasn't wry. Which was just fine with me.

"Have you had lunch? I've got a cheeseburger on the way."

"Actually, I haven't eaten."

I called a waitress over and Kathy ordered.

Kathy, I should finally get around to saying, was the editor of *Noir;* she was the very person who'd been doing those favorable reviews of my books. So naturally I respected her intellectually, being as how she had such high standards and good taste in matters literary (unless she panned my next book, in which case all bets were off). But I'd be lying if I didn't admit I was just as attracted to her physically as mentally.

Frankly, feeling attracted to Kathy, young, pert, pixie-fresh Kathy, helped flush the uncomfortable feeling I had about Mae Kane out of my system.

"I really like your magazine," I said, between bites of cheeseburger.

"You and our thousand or so other readers."

"You ought to have a better circulation than that."

"I know. It's that screwed-up publisher of mine."

I lifted my eyebrows and put 'em back down. "I'm glad you brought that up, not me."

"Oh, really?"

"Your publisher. Gregg Gorman. He's an s.o.b., you know."

Taking a bite of her own cheeseburger, she rolled her eyes and nodded, swallowed, said, "You're telling me. But he pays the bills, and stays out of my way."

"It's a nice little magazine."

"If Gregg'd just promote it, it could be a bigger nice little magazine. He's stubborn; he sells it to the mystery fan market, and won't bother trying for newsstand distribution. We've got articles, fiction by some up-and-coming writers—you wouldn't like to try a short story, would you?"

"Sure. What's your word rate?"

Her mouth and chin crinkled in embarrassment. "Half a cent per."

"Ouch. I always wanted to know what it felt like to be an old-time pulp writer."

"Now you'll know. Unless you're going to back out . . ."

"Well, I did say yes, so a deal's a deal."

Wry smile; rerun of the first one. "Anyway," she said, getting back on the track of an earlier train of thought, "*Noir*'s a slick little 'zine and Gorman's getting his books into Dalton's and Walden's and other outlets, so I keep nudging him to do something on a bigger scale with my little baby. But he doesn't."

"He's a man of vast imagination; some people see a sunset and just see a sunset—Gorman sees a sunset, and belches."

She nodded. "That's Gregg. He's a paternalistic little shit, is what he is, making passes at me every chance he gets."

"That's not something I want to hear about while I'm eating."

She waved a hand that had a little catsup on it. "Don't worry, Gregg's too much of a coward for there to be any gory anecdotes behind what I said. Fortunately we live half a continent apart and get together only rarely, and his come-ons are restricted primarily to the phone. But that's bad enough, believe me. He comes on to me in the sleazy, chauvinistic way that went out with Gat Garson."

I'd put Roscoe Kane's death almost out of mind, for a few minutes; her flip remark brought it back to me, and my face must've shown it, because she said, "Oh. I'm sorry. That wasn't in very good taste, was it? With Roscoe Kane dying last night and everything. I just could never read those stupid books, frankly."

A wall came up between us.

"I loved those books," I said. A little coldly.

She didn't pick up on the coldness. "That's just 'cause you're a man. You grew up in the '50s, and that was your era, and it hits you in a way that just goes right past me. I look at those macho private eye books and my stomach turns the corner, y'know?" She noticed the catsup on her hand and kissed it off; an unconsciously sexy little move. Seeing her do that, I would have had a hard time not warming back up to her. Which proved I was the chauvinistic boor she apparently suspected me of being.

Or did she?

"See," she was saying intensely, her dark eyes looking at me with a naïve sophistication, "your books are worlds apart from that tough-guy tripe. Your hero is sensitive. He thinks of women as persons, not sex objects ... he sees women as ..." And she looked upward for the word; while she did that I studied the word *Noir*. " . . . existential beings trapped in the same absurd world as he is. Don't you agree?"

I raised my eyes, if not my consciousness. I smiled at her. "Completely. Does this mean separate checks?"

She stopped and her face was a blank for a moment, and then one of her repertoire of wry smiles found its way to her face, and she said, "I sound like a pretentious jerk, don't I?"

I shrugged. "You sound like somebody who writes reviews for *Noir*."

"Is there a difference?"

"That depends," I said, placing tongue firmly in cheek, "on whether you're praising G. Pompous Donaldson, or me."

She shook her head, the smile shifting to one side of her face. "How a writer as sensitive as you can dislike Donaldson, and deify Kane, is beyond me."

"The last time anybody called me sensitive was when I got my flu shot. And how somebody as insightful as you can fall for Donaldson's bombastic claptrap is beyond yours truly, Johnny Dollar."

"Huh?"

"Old radio show. You're too young to remember it, and too literary to have heard of it. Listen, Donaldson's guy is named Keats—a private eye named after a poet! Gimme a break!"

"That's no more pretentious than calling your hero Mallory. That's a reference to Sir Thomas Malory, and *Morte d'Arthur*, I assume. Linking your hero to knights, rather obviously."

"Like hell! It's my name!"

"Oh. Well, why do you only use one name? You've got a first name, don't you?"

"People call me Mal."

"But that's short for 'Mallory.' What's more pompous than signing your work with one name?"

"Using a first initial, a middle and last name; or, God forbid, three names! Look, I have a first name, but nobody, including me, uses it, except on official documents."

"What is it, then?"

"Something that wouldn't sound good in print."

"It couldn't be *that* bad."

"Oh, no?"

"Oh, come on, tell me. What is it? I won't tell."

"Promise?"

"Promise."

"Not in *Noir?*"

"Nowhere."

I told her.

It sobered her.

"I see what you mean," she said. "Maybe just 'Mallory' *is* wiser."

"Perhaps in the future you'll learn to trust me. And my comments about Donaldson are also not for publication. Panning one of my peers in print is definitely not cool. Okay?"

"Sure," she said, sipping at her Coke with a straw, looking fifteen years old, making me glad she was really ten years older. "Still, you seem to have the sort of outspoken notions that *Noir* readers would get a kick out of reading about."

"I don't know . . ."

"Well, I do. I'd like to interview you, over the weekend, some time."

"I don't think so . . ."

"You can edit the rough copy, censor anything you like, if something you say looks stupid or harsh on paper."

"I'll think about it."

"Dinner still on?"

"You're from Pennsylvania someplace, aren't you?"

"Yeah. West Mifflin."

"Maybe I better introduce you to Chicago-style pizza, then. This evening."

Wry little grin #458. "Okay. Separate checks?"

"It'll be my treat," I said.

"Okay."

We stood; I pointed to the luncheon check. "You can get that one."

She laughed. "Fair enough. Heading back to the Congress?"

"Yeah. The dealers' room should just about be set up. I need to talk to that lovely publisher of yours, and he should be up there."

She paid at the register and we went out onto the street; there was a breeze, a breeze with a Chicago bite in it, and it was still foggy. I had a light jacket on, dug my hands in my pockets against the cold; she just had the sweatshirt, her breasts poking at the heavy cloth, dotting the eye in *Noir* a second time—being sensitive, I pretended not to notice. She pretended not to notice me pretending not to notice.

"Are you taking that Crime Tour this afternoon?" she asked; we were walking arm in arm—it was cold enough to justify that, even if our relationship wasn't that far along yet.

"What Crime Tour's that?"

"There's a bus tour of various famous Chicago crime scenes. Think of the history on view—the genre's dark roots revealed!"

"You really are the editor of *Noir*, aren't you?"

"Yeah, I am. You comin'?"

"I think I'll pass." I'd seen enough crime scenes for one weekend. "You can give me the full report tonight over pizza."

We stopped at a crosswalk; the Congress was just up ahead.

She looked sideways at me. "Say—what happened between you and Gregg, anyway?"

"Do I need a reason to loathe that guy?"

"No."

The light changed and we crossed.

"Well," I said, "it's a long story. I'll tell you sometime."

We went in the front hotel entrance, past the doorman through the revolving doors and up the interior ramp to the promenade of shops. A woman in her late fifties, heavy-set in a brown dress, rolled past like an orange-haired tank. Her face, which had been pretty once, was grim.

I stopped in my tracks.

Kathy went a couple steps beyond me, before she realized I'd been left behind; she glanced back with a look of exaggerated puzzlement.

"What's wrong, Mal?"

"Nothing. Go on up to the dealers' room, why don't you. I'll catch you later."

She shrugged, smirked wryly, and went on toward the bank of elevators.

I went in the other direction, toward the lobby, where I'd seen Roscoe Kane's second wife, Evelyn, heading.

7

EVELYN KANE was shouting at a pretty young black woman in a blazer behind the check-in counter; the clerk's face was as impassively attractive as Evelyn's was actively unattractive.

"Well, I want to *see* the son of a bitch!" Evelyn said. "When *will* he be on duty?"

"You'll have to speak to the manager," the woman said.

"Where *is* the manager?"

"He's not here at the moment."

"Well, when *will* he be here?"

"I don't know. You'll have to come back later, ma'am."

"What's your name, honey?" The honey held no affection.

The faintest of smirks hid in one corner of the black woman's mouth as she pointed to the name badge that said "Ms. Brown."

And Evelyn Kane turned, seething, and faced me.

"Just what I need," she said.

"Hello, Evelyn."

She pointed a finger at me; her face was a tight mask—like Jack Klugman suppressing gas. "I want to *talk* to you, pal."

"Fine. I wouldn't mind talking to you, either."

She began walking, toward the nearest exit, apparently; I fell in step.

Stamping on like a drill sergeant, she said, without looking at me, "You saw Roscoe last night, right?"

"Right."

"I want you to tell me all about it. All right?"

"All right," I shrugged.

"Let's have a drink, then."

I followed her out of the hotel; she stopped and stood just outside the doorway momentarily, as if daring the October breeze to faze her. It fazed me. I dug my hands in my pockets as I followed her down the street and around the corner to a sleazy little bar; the Americana-Congress was a relatively nice hotel, but you didn't have to walk far from it to find something sleazy—a fact of life in most of downtown Chicago, which seemed a study in side-by-side incongruities. Not the least of which were Evelyn Kane and I, seated now in a corner booth. She was presently answering a question I hadn't asked, explaining why we hadn't used one of the several bars in the hotel.

"I hate hotel bars," she said. "Expensive watered-down drinks and executives on expense accounts. Executives aren't people, you know—they used to be people, I suppose. But expense accounts turn people into leeches."

I liked the way Evelyn talked—she talked like a character in one of her ex-husband's books—but I didn't like Evelyn much.

"You don't like me much, do you?" she asked, smiling over the draw beer that had barely been set down in front of her before she scooped it up toward her face.

I sipped the Coke I'd ordered. "I think you're a peach, Evelyn. I'd give anything for a pin-up of you to hang over my bed."

She laughed and beer came out her nose. "I like you, kid. You got class."

"I always thought you hated my guts."

She shrugged; her eyes were elaborately laced with red, I noticed. "You came around and saw Roscoe and filled his head with how good he was. It was a bad time for him; right about the time he realized he wasn't going to get published anymore, not in the U.S., anyway. You had a bad effect on him."

"I thought I cheered him up."

"Sure. He'd get high off all your hero worship. Then he'd come down. Crash down. To reality. Which is a hell of a place for a writer to have to come, as you probably know. And, I felt you and some other people like you were leeches, looking for free writing help and advice and connections."

"Can I tell you why *I* think you didn't like me, Evelyn?"

"Can I stop you?"

"You were jealous. Your marriage was on the rocks, and I came around and got your husband's attention and it pissed you off."

She thought about that while she finished the beer. "You're right," she said, waving at the waitress for another. She'd been a waitress herself once but didn't seem to have any particular empathy for our suspiciously young one.

That's where she'd met Roscoe, back in Milwaukee in the '50s—waiting on him in a neighborhood bar. To hear Roscoe tell it, she'd been a bosomy, *zaftig* blonde, in those days; hard to imagine, looking at her faded orange hair and bearlike body and the face that had more wrinkles and folds than a suit of Goodwill clothes. Still, buried in that face were features that even now seemed pleasant if not pretty, if you dug for them hard enough. Maybe I *would* have enjoyed a pin-up of her over my bed, if it were of the right vintage.

Part of me wanted to like her. But I remembered how shrewish she'd been around Roscoe—and the impression I'd carried away from meeting her was that she was a lowlife who'd found a meal ticket, a blue-collar gold digger who turned not only fat but bitchy as the meal ticket started petering out.

Now, looking at this woman whose red eyes today came not entirely from drinking, I wondered if I might have misjudged her, at least a little.

"Looking back," she said, "I think what you gave Roscoe was a good thing. In the long term."

"What do you mean?"

"Well, the short term was a high followed by a crashin' low, yes. But over the long haul I think the correspondence with you and the visits from you built his confidence back up, kept his self-respect more or less in working order. So I want to apologize, Mallory. I was rude to you, way back when. Why don't we start over, you and me?"

I wondered why she was trying to get on my good side; I wondered it aloud, in fact.

"Looking for ulterior motives," she said. "Mystery writers are all alike. Being married to a writer is like being married to a psychiatrist. Remember the old joke about the psychiatrist who passes a guy on the street, and the guy says, 'Hello,' and the psychiatrist says to himself, 'I wonder what he meant by that?' That's what being married to one of you analytical sons of bitches is like. You keep trying to make sense out of your life. You keep looking for motivations and 'patterns of behavior,' when you deal with people. But life isn't like books. It's a goddamn mess, Mallory. It isn't tighty plotted; and people don't behave rationally. And things don't work out like they're supposed to."

Somewhere in the midst of that speech her red eyes began tearing up; and now, her speech finished, she stared into her beer and tears flowed.

"You must like salt in your beer," I said.

"Go to hell," she said, good-naturedly.

"You still love him, don't you?"

"Don't you?" she said.

Somebody dropped some money into a jukebox and Willie Nelson began to sing "Blue Skies."

"That's a great old song," she said.

"Maybe, but I don't like Willie Nelson."

"Listen to the *song*, you jerk. You claim to be a writer—listen to the words!" She sat for a moment, lost in the music. Almost wistfully she added, "He sings it real nice, too. That Willie Nelson. What a singer. What a man. Somethin' about him always reminds me of Roscoe."

"Yeah," I said. "They both look like they fell off a lumber wagon."

That amused her; she didn't laugh out loud, but she laughed.

"We should've been pals, Mallory."

"Maybe it's not too late."

"Maybe not. Why don't you tell me about seeing Roscoe last night."

"I'll get to that. First tell me what that Abbott and Costello routine you were doing with the girl at the front desk at the hotel was about?"

Intensity tightened her sagging face. "I want to talk to the night man. The assistant manager who found my husband's body."

83

"That guy wasn't who found the body."

"Yeah, well, the bitch found him. But the night man was first on the scene after that."

"By the bitch, I take it you mean Mae."

"Mae, the bitch, right. The home-wrecking god-damn bitch."

Funny hearing Evelyn call Mae that, considering Evelyn seduced Roscoe away from his first (now late) wife.

"Actually, the night guy was *third* on the scene," she said. "I understand somebody else was with the bitch when she found Roscoe, but I can't seem to find out who—that's one thing the night manager can tell me, who the guy was that was with her. Somebody she was humping, no doubt. Him, I want to talk to, also."

"Evelyn, *I* was with Mae when she found Roscoe."

Her eyes got very alert. "Oh. I didn't know that."

"You do now." I told her about it, but tried to downplay my suspicions. It didn't take.

"Your instincts are right," she said.

"What do you mean?"

"He *was* murdered."

"How can you be so sure?"

She hesitated. "Roscoe was on the verge of something big."

I sat forward. "What do you mean?"

"Maybe I'll tell you." She bit her lip. "But not right now. I gotta think it through, first."

"If you know something that will help convince the authorities that this is—or at least *might* be—a murder, then don't hold back, Evelyn. Tell me what you know."

She smiled, but the smile was oddly private. "Don't give me that. I read your books, pal."

"What's that supposed to mean?"

84

"Just that. I read 'em. Roscoe loaned 'em to me. He was proud of you. You were his prize pupil. And only."

A wave of emotion ran through me; I swallowed and tried to keep my own beer from getting salty.

I said, "I still don't see what that has to do . . ."

"Those stories of yours, those books, were *true*, weren't they?"

"More or less."

"That's what I thought," she said smugly.

"Make your point, Evelyn."

"I didn't like the books."

"So?"

"The writing seemed okay; I'm no writer, but I lived with one long enough to know writing when I see it. I just didn't like what you did with it. I didn't like you taking those two real murders you happened to fall into and turnin' 'em into mystery stories. It's like I said, writers are always trying to turn real life into stories, nice 'n' tidy with beginnings and middles and ends, and real life isn't like that. And, frankly, pal, I think you were kind of a leech, turnin' those real-life tragedies into something you could make a buck off of."

"Your disapproval is noted, Evelyn. But what's that got to do with what happened to Roscoe?"

She gave me a nasty smile over the lip of her beer glass. "My point is your amateur detective crap won't cut it here. You're in Chicago; and you're in over your head. This should be left to the police, kiddo."

"I'd love to leave it to the police. Unfortunately nobody but me is convinced Roscoe's death was murder."

"I'm convinced. And I'll talk to the police about it, soon enough. But this is *my* business, Mallory. I'll handle this *my* way, 'cause I'm involved, and you're

85

not; 'cause I know what's going on, and you don't have a clue. So take my motherly advice and keep out."

"Oh, really?"

"Find some other murder to write your next book about."

Liking Evelyn had been a short-term event.

"What are you *doing* here, anyway?" I snapped at her. "Did you come down from Milwaukee this morning when you heard the news of Roscoe's death, or what?"

She drank some beer. "I was already coming down. I heard about it on the radio coming down, in fact."

"*Why* were you coming down?"

"To meet Roscoe, of course."

"Evelyn—you and Roscoe were divorced a long, long time ago. With little love lost."

She jerked upright in the booth; the beer in her hand splashed. "You don't know my life. You didn't write my life, I'm not a character in one of your goddamn books. So don't go making . . . pronouncements . . . about me or my life!"

"Okay, okay. Maybe that was out of line. But what . . . business did you have here with Roscoe?"

She smiled enigmatically. "It *was* partly business. But it was mostly love."

The jukebox started in on "Blue Skies" again.

"Love?"

"Roscoe and I were getting back together. He was planning to divorce Mae."

"Oh, come on, Evelyn . . ."

She looked hurt; defensive. Suddenly the pretty woman she had once been became more apparent; the fat old woman faded for an instant, and the ghost of the *zaftig* blonde asserted itself.

"You think you know so much about Roscoe Kane," she said. "Well, here's something you didn't know: we'd been having an affair the past six months. The bitch thought ol' Gat Garson couldn't get it up anymore, but he got it up for me just fine. Pick up the check, would you, honey?"

And she was up and out of there, moving faster than a big woman like her had any right to, and by the time I paid the check and went out after her, she was gone.

8

I RODE the escalator up to the hotel's second floor,
where the dealers' room was, feeling dazed, even a
little battered, from my confrontation with Evelyn
Kane. I didn't know what to make of much of what
she'd said; her revelation about having an affair with
her ex-husband seemed like lunacy. That didn't mean
it might not be true, of course. I had just checked at
the front desk and Evelyn Kane had not—at least not
yet—checked in at the Americana-Congress. She'd
disappeared in a cloud of hot air—which was what
her story about getting back together with Roscoe
had to be. Didn't it?

The 'con registration desk was a long banquet table
against the wall at the top of the escalator. The two
young women and the young man behind the table
were mystery fans enlisted for this dirty work, and
they were eagerly chattering about the mystery writers they'd been meeting. They put me in my place by
having obviously never heard of me. I had prepaid,
so all I had to do was check in, pick up my plastic
name badge, pin it to my sweater and be humiliated
by the lack of recognition. Bouchercon was under
way for me.

The dealers' room (which actually sprawled over several rooms adjacent to the large Gold Room, site of most of the 'con's major activities) hadn't been open long and some of the dealers were still in the process of setting up. The Mystery House table was one of the latter, and one of Gorman's flunkys was doing the setting up, a thin, acned kid in a plaid shirt; the enormous pleasure of seeing Gregg Gorman himself would have to wait.

Friday was never a terribly active day at a Bouchercon—only the professional writers and diehard fans who'd flown or driven in from here/there/everywhere would be around; Saturday would find Chicago-area fans flocking to a complete card of activities—speakers, panel discussions, movies—and Bouchercon, Chicago-Style, would be in full swing.

Still, there were probably twenty-five or thirty people wandering about the room, and the number of dealer tables was probably nearly the same. I bumped into Sardini and Murtz, both of whom carried ever-growing stacks of books they'd just bought, each commenting about having to go home after the 'con and immediately write and sell something to make up for what they'd been spending. Some of the dealers were hawking new books by the likes of Donald E. Westlake, Joe Gores and Lawrence Block—as well as studies and biographies on writers like Rex Stout, Dorothy Sayers and John D. MacDonald. And of course there were books by the writers who'd be appearing at the 'con, which gave fans a chance to pick up copies to get autographed. Cynthia Crystal was sitting at a table doing just that with her Hammett bio, for a cluster of fans of various ages and sexes (all wearing glasses—see what reading gets you?). Several dealers were carrying my books, and I thanked them for their support; most dealers are mystery *fans* as well, and a couple had copies of my two novels tucked away for an autograph, which I gladly gave them. If only the guy at the Port City Seven-Eleven who always insisted on seeing my ID before cashing my checks could see me now . . .

The major attraction of the room, however, was old books: hardcover editions in dustjacket, with prices routinely in the forty to one hundred dollar area—*The Long Goodbye* by Raymond Chandler, a surrealistic cover depicting a little idol with blood on it; *Galatea* by James M. Cain, a purple cover with a picture of a water tower. The appeal of all this was a bit beyond me. I've never been a collector, anyway not the type who has to have first editions and the like (a novel's a novel—it doesn't matter to me what's on the cover or what edition it is, so long as it's in English). But I did get a kick out of seeing the rare old paperbacks from the '40s and '50s, with their garish covers.

I had done my collecting years and years ago, in secondhand stores where I'd gotten dog-eared paperbacks of Spillane and Prather and Roscoe Kane and the like with gloriously tacky covers, babes and bullets and blood—what more could an impressionable teenager ask? And I'd paid a nickel or a dime apiece for them. The dealers here were asking (and sometimes getting) ten dollars and up. It wasn't unusual to see a paperback (*The Marijuana Mob* by James Hadley Chase; *Five Murderers* by Raymond Chandler) go for thirty dollars or more.

And all the Roscoe Kane first edition paperbacks—which yesterday would have brought perhaps five dollars per—were marked twenty-five dollars and up. Dying can do wonders for a guy's career. Gat Garson would've cheerfully shot the dealers who'd indulged in this overnight grave robbing; Gat wasn't around, so I shot them for him—using dirty looks for ammunition, instead of .38 slugs. Not that any of them noticed, or anyway cared.

I caught up with Kathy and her *Noir* sweatshirt at a table where a lavish paperback selection had every passerby's eyes popping out at the bright colors and sexy, gory subject matter. This particular dealer was a guy I knew—Bob Weinberg, a bearded guy with glasses and a sense of humor so dry you didn't laugh till a day later; his prices today were, as usual, not out of line. And he hadn't raised his Roscoe Kane prices, either. I complimented him on that.

"Don't be silly," he said. He wore a green sweater and cream button-down shirt and gray slacks, a conservative contrast to the excesses of the covers of his wares, spread out before him like a kitsch banquet. (Do real men eat kitsch?)

"It's just refreshing to run across a dealer who isn't a ghoul."

"Dealers are rumored to be human," he said, as if not entirely in agreement with that notion. "I do have a Roscoe Kane item you might be interested in. In fact, I brought it with you in mind."

"I have all the books, Bob. And I don't have the patience to go after the short stories in the pulps."

"No, this is something special. I think you'll like this. Let me check with my wife and see where we put it."

Bob's wife was his business partner.

Meanwhile, Kathy was looking at the cover of a Kane book called *Hearse Class Frail*.

"Don't tell anybody," she said, "but I have to admit I like these covers."

This particular one portrayed a beautiful busty blonde in a negligee looking out her bedroom window

91

where, in the blue darkness of the night, Gat Garson was punching out several thugs.

"You don't like the books," I said, "but you like the covers."

She shrugged. "It evokes an era. And I have to admit something . . ."

"Feel free."

"I never read one of these Gat Garson things all the way through. Maybe if I got into one . . ."

"I'll buy you a copy of one of his better ones."

"That'd be nice. I'd like to give Roscoe Kane another try."

"As a gesture to me."

She gave me wry smile #764. "Maybe I'm just trying to keep on your good side. I'm counting on that interview with you."

"Your publisher might have some objection to your running an interview with me, you know."

"Gregg gives me free editorial rein. The interview's still on, then?"

"Sure. Why not?"

"After you take me out to dinner, that is."

"Right. I'm all for bribing journalists before they interview me; it's good for my image."

"What image is that?"

I scowled at her. "The Gat Garson of the '80s."

Weinberg was back and he had a big twenty-by-twenty-five piece of bristol board covered with a protective sheet of tissue paper through which I could, barely, see something—something I liked very much.

"I don't collect that stuff," I said, not very convincingly.

"It's up to you," Weinberg said. Not the hardest sell.

"It's beautiful," Kathy said, something like awe in her voice.

And so it was: the original cover painting to *Murder Me Again, Doll*, my favorite Gat Garson novel; the very painting that had adorned the cover of the novel's original publication in 1958, which I had read a battered used copy of in 1961, the first Roscoe Kane novel I ever read, the book that gave me Gat Garson fever.

The painting showed Gat on a fire escape, a lithe brunette beauty in a negligee huddling next to him as he fired his .38 down toward several armed thugs climbing up toward them. It was a night scene, blue tones shattered by bursts of red and orange from Gat's gat.

"It's by Kinstler," Weinberg said. "He's a big-time portrait painter now, you know—his paperback covers are getting collectible."

"I believe it."

"Imagine," Weinberg said, "having a painting by somebody who did both Gerald Ford's portrait *and* Gat Garson's."

"I don't think I can afford it." I was holding the painting in my hands, which were shaking—Gat seemed to be moving; I could almost hear the gun going KA-*CHOW* . . . .

"I was going to ask two hundred for it. Unless you wanted it, in which case I'd settle for one seventy-five. Of course, that was before Roscoe Kane died on us."

"*Now* what do you want?"

"One seventy-five."

"It might be worth twice that, now that Roscoe's gone."

"I brought it here to offer you for one seventy-five. Do you want it or not?"

I handed the painting back to him—and wrote him out a check.

"Keep it for me till I've been around the room, would you, Bob?"

"Sure," he said—shrugging, as if this deal couldn't have meant less to him. But he'd gone out of his way to be nice to me, and had managed to confirm the rumor that some dealers *were* human, after all.

Kathy and I walked along, glancing at the various tables of colorful paperback and pulp covers.

"Did you notice how much the 'doll' Gat's holding onto in the painting looked like you?" I asked her.

"I was afraid to point it out without sounding like an egomaniac," she admitted. "That's some pretty girl in that painting."

"Don't you mean pretty 'woman'?"

Her smile went crinkly on me. "No, Mal. That was definitely a girl."

"You, on the other hand, are . . ."

"Definitely a woman. But is that so bad?"

"You don't hear me complaining."

We each picked up a few books as we wandered through the adjacent rooms—she bought an extra copy of guest-of-honor Donaldson's most recent novel, *Poisonous Wine*, to get an autograph later; and I found a couple of novels I'd been looking for by Jim Thompson, an underappreciated crime novelist of the '50s whose bleak books made James M. Cain seem like Louisa May Alcott. Phyllis White, the widow of the 'con's namesake, Anthony Boucher, and a regular, treasured guest of the Bouchercon, was chatting with Otto Penzler at the Mysterious Press table. Kathy and I stopped so I could pick up the Spillane collection Penzler had recently published and I exchanged smiles with Otto and Mrs. White. Tim Culver had joined Cynthia at the autograph table; they were cordial to the fans, but I still sensed a tension between them.

Then we came to the Mystery House table. Various Gorman publications were on display—including that slipcased set of Carroll John Daly that both Tom Sardini and I had sprung for by mail—and so was Gorman.

So much for dealers being human.

I hadn't noticed him come in, which was like failing to notice a garbage scow pull into your marina. I must've been caught up in that deal with Weinberg and the painting, and Gorman must've been uncharacteristically close-mouthed for the past few minutes, because normally his loud and obnoxious voice would have carried like a bad smell in a small room.

"Well," he said. "It's Mallory. The asshole."

He wasn't a big man, at least not tall; maybe five-eight. He had a beer belly and a goatee in which flecks of his last half-dozen meals hung on like bad memories. His hair was a washed-out, colorless red and thinning, and his nose was roadmapped darker red. His eyes were little dark beady things that looked out from under bushy eyebrows like bugs hiding under weeds. His thick upper lip curled up under the mustache part of the goatee and revealed teeth as yellow as the sun, but not shining.

"I love you, too, Gorman."

He poked a thumb at a chest ensconced in a pale green sweater polka-dotted with vague foodstains and strained to the point of looking threadbare over the protruding belly; one of the collars of the paisley shirt beneath the sweater poked out like a knife, the other was tucked in. For a guy worth half a million easy, he was hardly a page out of *GQ*.

"Anytime you want a piece of me, say the word, asshole. We can step outside now, if you like."

"All right," I said.

95

He just stood there behind his table with a nervous, fallen expression, trying to figure out what to do since I'd called his bluff.

Then he grinned, lamely. "You'd fall for anything, Mallory. You're that big a sucker."

"Oh. I get it. You were just kidding. You don't want to go outside and beat me up."

"I got better things to do."

"Like swindle people?" I said.

He bristled. "That's a serious accusation, asshole. You . . . you better be able to back that up."

I looked at Kathy, whose presence Gorman hadn't yet acknowledged despite her being the editor of one of his publications, and said, "You want to hear why the king of Publisher's Row, here, doesn't like me?"

Caught between me and her boss, Kathy just looked blank, managing to swallow once, but not to say anything.

I went ahead: "There was an old mystery writer named Raoul Wheeler. He wasn't the greatest mystery writer in the world, but he did a series of short stories back in the '40s about a character who was the forerunner of James Bond. Erik Flayr, a secret service man who battled larger-than-life villains."

Kathy was nodding; she'd heard of Wheeler and his creation.

Despite her knowing most of this, I wanted to say it all; some people were gathering, and not all of them knew the Raoul Wheeler story.

"Wheeler was one of those writers like Carroll John Daly who are historically important, mentioned in all the reference books and such, but who didn't *really* make it. The Flayr character had a brief period of popularity in the pulps, and Columbia Pictures even made a serial about him; but that was it for Wheeler— his moment of glory. Then came the James Bond boom in the '60s and some of the mystery-fiction historians remembered Wheeler's work and started dropping his name. But none of Wheeler's Eric Flayr stuff got brought back in print, during the Bond boom, because Wheeler had never done Flayr novels, just short stories, and publishers of paperbacks like to do novels, not short-story collections. . . ."

The rest of Gorman's face was gradually turning to the same shade of red as his nose.

"Wheeler finished out his career writing soft-core porn and confession-magazine stuff, never amounting to much . . . but he had a certain pride in Eric Flayr. He lived in Clinton, Iowa, Wheeler did, near me. I heard he was living there and I drove up to meet him. He lived in a two-room flat and he was ill—dying of cancer, in fact. A frail little man with a mustache. Skinny. But he was a nice old guy, with lots of stories about people he met in the pulp days—Hammett, Chandler, Daly, Fred Nebel, Frank Gruber, all those guys—and he had a complete collection of the *Thrilling Detective Adventure* pulps with his Eric Flayr stories in them. One afternoon, he gave them to me. A gift. A legacy."

Gorman began talking to his flunky, that teen-aged kid with acne on his neck and a plaid shirt. Pretending to ignore me, and the small crowd that was gathering.

"I was an innocent back then—this was maybe six years ago. All I knew about Gregg Gorman was that he was reprinting rare, important mystery fiction, for the hard-core mystery fan market. So I wrote him a letter. Told him I had a complete run of the Flayr stories. Suggested collecting them into a book. Gorman called me—he came on a little strong, but I figured that was just the difference between Chicago and Port City, Iowa. What did I care if he was obnoxious, as long as he published a collection of

Wheeler's stories—which he said he intended doing. In fact, he'd had the idea before I even came to him, but had been stopped by the rarity of this particular pulp—even top collectors like Blackbeard and Pronzini didn't have a complete run of *Thrilling Detective Adventures* between them! So he was very grateful."

Gorman quit pretending not to be paying attention and tried to stare me down.

"We met in Chicago and worked out a deal: I would provide him with photocopies of all the stories—they numbered forty-some in all—and he agreed to pay Wheeler an advance of a thousand dollars per book . . . he planned a series of four Eric Flayr collections. And while four thousand dollars isn't the moon, it would mean a lot to Wheeler, both financially and in terms of building his self-esteem by showing him that something he'd written had enough lasting value to generate a few bucks for him, at this late stage of the game. Also, Gorman agreed to put my name on the cover as editor of the series, use introductions by me, and pay me a hundred dollars per book. This meant quite a bit to me at the time, because I hadn't published anything more than a few short stories in *Mike Shayne's Mystery Magazine*, and I could use the exposure."

"Get out of here," Gorman said. "You're blocking my table—I wanna do some business here!"

"The punchline is predictable. Gorman looked into the copyright on the *Thrilling Detective Adventure* material and found it had lapsed; this made the Eric Flayr stories public domain. He used the photocopied material I provided to put the books together, and paid neither Wheeler nor myself a cent."

Gorman said, "You didn't have a contract, asshole."

I pointed a finger at him. "Call me that *once* more."

He sneered at me, but didn't say anything.

"Wheeler died before the first of the books came out," I told her—and the little crowd. "And Gorman here built his publishing empire on it."

"Empire," Gorman snorted. "I'm just a small-businessman, a cottage industry, and a fan who likes mysteries. Who besides me woulda printed that old hack's garbage? *I* gave him some posterity, schmuck. You're just cryin' 'cause I didn't put your name on the covers."

I said nothing.

The crowd began to disperse—a crowd of people shaking their heads.

"Thanks, jerk," he said. "I oughta sue you for defamation of character."

"You'll have to come up with some character, first," I said.

Besides—these fans wouldn't boycott Gorman; even *I* bought Gorman's books, though I did so through another dealer, so as not to give him the satisfaction of knowing he was getting my money. For all his faults, Gorman was one of a handful of publishers putting out books of rare material the fans sorely wanted; and he *was* the publisher who had resurrected the Eric Flayr tales from their unjust oblivion. He was also the first American publisher in over a decade to give Roscoe Kane's work the light of day. . . .

"I want to talk to you about Roscoe Kane," I said.

"Screw you," he said.

"I have to admit I'm glad to hear you'll be doing Roscoe's final few Garson books."

"First in the U.S. to do it," he said smugly.

"Maybe with the publicity Roscoe's death'll generate, you'll have a valuable piece of property in those books."

"What's that supposed to mean?"

"Just an observation."

"Get outta here, Mallory! Just get the hell away."
He looked at Kathy. "You're not with *him*, are you?"

Kathy, stunned by the behavior of both of us, managed only to nod.

"You keep lousy company, baby," he said to her.

She burned. "It's nothing compared to my taste in publishers," she said, and turned and walked quickly away.

I pointed a finger at Gorman again. "We're going to talk some more," I said.

"I'm shakin', I'm shakin'," Gorman said, moving his body like a little kid responding to threats from another little kid. Which was maybe the case.

When I caught up with Kathy, she glared at me. "Couldn't that have waited?"

"Uh, what have waited?"

"Your big scene with Gorman. He *is* my boss, you know!"

"Come on—that guy's an iguana. He's . . ."

"My publisher!" She turned and gave me a tight angry look. "*Noir* means a lot to me. I don't make much off it, it's not my living, you understand, but it's the part of my life that makes the rest of my life worth living. And Gorman's my publisher. He may not be Hugh Hefner, but he's my publisher!"

"He isn't even Larry Flynt, Kathy."

"I don't care! You could've had the courtesy to pull that stunt without me at your side! It was thoughtless!"

I sighed. "Yeah. I guess it was. Sorry."

"Just leave me alone."

She walked toward the elevators.

She pressed the UP button and stood with folded arms. I came up to her and said, "Is supper still on?"

Her reply about snapped my head off: "Why? Do you want to back out?"

"No."

"Me, neither," she said and stepped into the elevator, and I caught a wisp of yet another wry smile before the doors slid shut.

9

I RESTED the cover painting of *Murder Me Again, Doll* against the wall next to the bed in my hotel room; I left the tissue paper over it but the garish cover beneath shouted through and reminded me of Roscoe Kane. I turned it to the wall, wondering if buying the thing had been a mistake.

No, I said to myself, someday the ugly circumstances surrounding Roscoe Kane's death will fade, and Kane, the writer, and Gat Garson, the character, would move to the forefront, pushing all the rest of it into the background, where it belonged. Then I could enjoy my painting. . . .

After all, I was able to listen to Beatles music again, wasn't I? I could hear "Hard Day's Night" or "Eight Days a Week" on the radio, and smile and sing along. One night, not so long ago, a news bulletin had interrupted the old Mamie Van Doren movie I was watching (*Sex Kittens Go to College*), and I knew at once that from then on I'd never be able to watch Mamie Van Doren without thinking of John Lennon, and, more importantly, would never be able to listen to Beatles music again, not with any joy anyway. . . .

But that, too, had passed; and now Beatles music, and various other music from my junior high and high school days, was about all I could stand to listen to; that and some of the new music that harked back to those days. I had a little Sony cassette player along, as a matter of fact, which was sitting on the hotel-room dresser at the moment, and I popped a tape in—a Bobby Darin tape—and fell back on the bed and tried to relax and forget about Roscoe Kane for a while.

But Bobby Darin wouldn't let me.

"*Splish splash,*" he sang, "*I was takin' a bath . . .*"

I sat up.

"Very funny, Bobby," I said, and got up and shut off the little cassette player.

And called Mae Kane's room.

"Y-yes . . . ?" she said, tentatively. From the sound of her voice—not to mention the eight rings she'd let go by before picking up the receiver—I could tell she'd had her share of calls from the media and condolence-wishers and such, and was getting gun-shy.

"Mae, it's Mal."

The voice went warm, husky. "Mal. Where are you calling from?"

"My room."

"You should've just stopped by, up here, if you wanted to talk. I could use the company. I've had to take all my meals in; room service here's my best friend."

I didn't want to go up to her room, partially because I didn't trust myself around her, sexually speaking—and I didn't exactly trust her, either, since maybe she spoke the same language.

But I didn't say that.

I said, "I ran into Evelyn Kane a while ago."

There was a long pause, a pregnant pause—but I didn't have to wait nine months to find out what the pause was pregnant with: hate. Hate that streamed out of the receiver like heat from a hair dryer.

Only, Mae's clipped words were more like ice.

"What's that bitch doing here?" she said.

She and Evelyn spoke the same language, too.

"Be fair, Mae. She *was* Roscoe's wife, once upon a time. She has a right to show her concern."

"Then she can come to the services Monday in Milwaukee; there's nothing for her here."

"You may be right. Tell me, had she and Roscoe gotten together in recent months?"

There was a wariness in her voice as she said, "What do you mean?"

I was obviously getting into an awkward area. "Oh, you know," I stumbled, trying to make it sound light. "Got together for old times. Mended some fences. Buried the hatchet. Bygones be bygones. That sort of thing."

"Well." She paused again, and the hate was gone, or anyway in check; she was composing herself. "I do think he saw her a few times. He ran into her once, at a grocery store or something. And they apparently were civil. They met for drinks once or twice after that. The marriage . . . ended pretty bitterly, as you may recall. Maybe . . . maybe they felt that after all these years, they should at least be civil."

"And that's as far as it went?"

"Of course. Where else could it go?"

"Evelyn claimed . . . look, I don't know if I should get into this. This isn't really any of my business. . . ."

Mae laughed and there was a tinge of sarcasm in it. "When did that ever stop you?" There was a tinge of gin in it, too; room service here *was* her best friend.

"You've got me there. What she said was—she said she and Roscoe were having an affair."

104

Silence.

"Mae?"

Silence.

And then an outburst of uproarious laughter.

"Mae?" I said, into the receiver, talking over the continuing laughter.

Finally she managed to contain her glee long enough to say, "That's rich. Oh, that's really rich."

"Can I take your hysteria as a 'no'?"

"Mal, you've seen us, Evelyn and me. Who would you rather . . .?" She hadn't had enough gin yet to complete *that* sentence. But she picked right up: "You knew Roscoe pretty well. What do you think? Do you think he was cheating on me to climb in bed with Madame LaFarge?"

"Mae, he was married to her once. He probably loved her, once. Love's blind."

"Maybe, but it's not retarded. Mal, she's a crazy, vicious bitch. What's next, a will leaving our bungalow to her, written in Crayola? She's a lunatic. Roscoe was nice to her because she was down on her luck; he felt sorry for her. Maybe—maybe he even felt a little guilty for having dumped her. Roscoe had his deep dark depressions, you know. He carried guilt around over both Evelyn and Winnie."

Winnie was Winifred, Roscoe's first wife, dead for many, many years.

"So," I said, "renewing his relationship with Evelyn was an act of charity on his part."

"Mal, he had drinks with her a few times. A relationship it wasn't."

"Mae. This is hard to ask."

"Somehow I think you'll find a way . . ."

"You indicated you and Roscoe weren't, well—sexually active, of late."

"He was impotent, Mal."

"Couldn't that have been the pose of a man carrying on an affair with another woman?"

"Mal! Jesus. He had prostate trouble, which is a matter of medical record, all right? Do I really have to go into this further?"

"No," I said, wishing there was a rock around to crawl under.

"Besides, if Roscoe wanted to leave me, all he had to do was do it. Roscoe and I have—had—a few thousand dollars in savings and own our little home. There wasn't enough there to bother fighting over. Mal, Evelyn Kane is a crazy woman. Why listen to her?"

"Mae. You agreed it would be a good idea for me to ask around about Roscoe's death. And Evelyn *is* here."

"True. Sorry. I didn't mean to snap at you."

"That's okay. I deserved it, a little."

"When did she get here, Mal?"

"Pardon?"

"Evelyn. When did she arrive?"

"Today. She said."

"Where do you suppose she was last night?"

"That I don't know. That's a good question. Of course I don't know where she is now, either."

"Why?"

I explained that Evelyn hadn't checked in at the Americana-Congress, at least not as of an hour or so ago.

"She might be at another hotel, though," I said. "With the convention, here, the hotel itself may be full."

"She's probably sleeping in her car," Mae said, humorously. "She's one classy broad."

"You said before that you could tell me where I could get hold of Roscoe's son," I reminded her.

"Jerome?" She laughed; almost a giggle. "Why, I'm sure you could get hold of him any place you pleased. No problem."

"Mae, take it easy on that gin, okay?"

"That *was* nasty, wasn't it? Jerome is staying with a Troy something. I've got it written down...."

She found the name and number and gave it to me, then asked, "Have you called that assistant coroner yet?"

"Actually, no. I'm going to do that after we hang up."

"Good. How about dinner tonight?"

"No, Mae, thank you. I already have a, uh ..."

"Previous engagement? Anyone I know?"

"I don't think so. A young lady."

"I'm jealous," she said, pretending not to be. "You could've had room service with me." She said that flatly, without stressing the innuendo—but the "nuendo" was in there, all right.

"That would've been nice," I managed.

"Maybe you can stop up later."

"I'll try." No way!

"Particularly if you get anywhere, with your inquiries."

"You'll be the first to know."

"Thanks, Mal. I know I can count on you."

"I'll call you later, that I promise you."

"Please do, Mal."

We hung up.

I called the Chicago coroner's office and managed to get Myers, the heavyset assistant coroner from last night. I reminded him who I was and he grunted, and I told him about the maid and the wet towels, and he said, That's very interesting, thank you, and hung up.

Which is how I knew he'd react, but I'd promised Mae I'd pass my wet-towel information along, and I had.

I called the front desk and asked if Evelyn Kane had checked in; she hadn't. I asked if she had a reservation; she hadn't. I asked if the hotel was full up, what with the convention and all; it was.

That certainly explained Evelyn's absence. Or did it? If she was planning ahead to come down from Milwaukee to see Roscoe, why didn't she have a reservation at the hotel?

I tried calling the number of Jerome Kane's friend, Troy. I got an answering machine, a very masculine voice saying, "This is Troy, I'm not able to respond at the moment, but please leave a message at the tone." Behind the voice, an instrumental version of the theme from the movie *Arthur* was playing; I didn't leave a message—I hung up when I was between the moon and New York City, actually.

I needed to talk to Gorman. I had blown it, sort of, down in the dealers' room; I should've played like all was forgiven between ol' Gregg and me, so I could sneak up on him with some hard questions, not the least of which was, Where the hell were *you* last night when Roscoe died, Gorman?

Now I had to wait for a better time and place, ideally somewhere I could get Gorman alone.

What I wanted to do now was talk to Roscoe's son, Jerome, but he and Troy were out.

So I slept for a while; not long.

Because less than ten minutes later someone started knocking on my door, and when I went to answer it, I found on my doorstep a tall, thin, tanly handsome man in his forties, his hair stark white in a short, stylish cut, wearing a beige suit with a light blue

108

open-collar shirt and one slender, elegant gold chain looping gently down across a hairless chest.

The face was familiar, though I'd never met this man.

The face was Roscoe Kane's.

Or at least it was Roscoe Kane's face before time and booze and gravity had got to it and basset-houndized it. The china-blue eyes were exactly Roscoe's.

A tapered hand extended itself and I took it, shook it; a firm handshake.

"Sorry we have to meet under such tragic circumstances, Mr. Mallory," he said, in a manner that seemed to me to be feigning more sorrow than he really felt. "I'm—"

"I know who you are," I said. "Troy's friend."

10

WE sat one table away from the table I'd shared with his father in the bar the night before. A few familiar faces were around—Tom Sardini and Peter Christian were nearby, part of a large party of writers, a few of whom I knew, but I didn't have to know each of 'em to tell they were writers—lots of beards and longish hair and glasses and slightly off-kilter clothing; we were a recognizable breed. I lacked the beard and mustache, but there'd been a time, back when Woodstock wasn't just a character in *Peanuts*, when I'd had facial fur, too. The vaguely unconventional look of the mystery writers my age echoed, however faintly, the left wing stand so many of us took in those Kent State days. Some of us voted straight Republican now (not me, but some of us did), yet the generation we were part of lingered in our appearance. We tended to look like assistant professors on small college campuses—the sort who never get elected department chairman, and only grudgingly, via tenure, achieve full professorship.

Anyway, Tom and Pete waved at me to join them, and I waved and smiled no, as nicely as possible, and turned my attention to Jerome Kane.

Jerome wasn't Woodstock generation; he was of that vague, Eisenhower/Howdy Doody generation that was just young enough to miss out on Korea and just old enough to avoid Vietnam. A conservative era; a safe era. But an era that produced its share of misfits— misfits, at least, by the standards of that day. Today, in the hip '80s, we don't consider homosexuals misfits—do we, Mr. Falwell?

I wasn't a born-again Christian, but I didn't like Jerome Kane, anyway. He'd been soft-spokenly polite in the elevator; his manners were impeccable, his manner graceful, not exactly effeminate. Any residue of bigotry against gays I might feel was not—I didn't think—a part of my instinctive dislike for him. Dislike? Too strong a word. Resentment. I resented this man.

Why?

"I envy you," he said. Suddenly.

We'd ordered drinks—he ordered Scotch and tonic, like his father, and I opted for a Coke, avoiding liquor to keep my head clear, seeking caffeine to keep me revved up. But we'd sat silently, waiting for the drinks to arrive; I had questions for him, but he'd called this meeting, so to speak, so I wanted him to speak first. I'd let him have the lead till it struck my fancy to take it from him.

Now, suddenly, he envied me.

"Why?" I said.

"You knew my father in a way I never could. Never will."

"Your father and I weren't really all that close."

The drinks came. A pretty barmaid even bustier than the one the night before gave me a generous view as she deposited the drinks on the table. I smiled at the barmaid and she smiled politely, and then I realized I was overcompensating, and felt foolish. I

111

was sitting at a table with a homosexual and I felt compelled to assert my heterosexuality.

The china-blue eyes smiled. "Attractive young lady."

"You noticed, did you?"

"I'm gay, not blind. And how do you know I don't appreciate the fairer sex, from time to time? Haven't you heard of bisexuals, in Iowa?"

"No, but I've heard of them in California."

"*Touché*. As I was saying."

"What *were* you saying?"

"You don't like me, do you, Mr. Mallory?"

"That isn't what you were saying."

"It's what you've been saying."

"I don't remember saying much of anything."

"That's precisely how you said it."

"Spare me the California mellow-speak, would you?"

"Is that what you call it in Iowa?"

"Actually, we call it bullshit. I'm just being polite."

"Ah, yes. Contempt is so often expressed by mock-civility."

I sipped my Coke. "Go to hell, Jerome."

Lids half hid the china-blue eyes. "I'm interested. What is it about me you dislike so? My sexual preferences wouldn't matter much to you, I'm guessing."

"That's right."

"What is it, then?"

I looked for a fast answer; any smart-ass remark to lob the ball back to him. But I couldn't find one.

And he just sat there staring at me with his father's eyes coming out of that tan face, the subdued lights in the place catching his droopy gold chain and tossing it at me.

Finally I said, "I don't know. I don't know why I don't like you. You seem decent enough. I think I maybe . . . resent your lack of appreciation of your father, for who he is . . . was."

112

"Is that all?"

"Well. I think you pose, a little . . ."

"Don't *you*? Don't you confuse yourself a bit with that sensitive latterday Philip Marlowe you portray in your books?"

"No. I know where fiction ends and reality begins."

"Oh, really? And where is that?"

"Somewhere east of San Francisco."

A smile crinkled one corner of his mouth and both his eyes. "Now you sound like a latter-day Gat Garson."

That made me smile. I'd have to be careful or I'd start liking this guy.

"You've read your father's books?" I asked.

He nodded. "Yes, I have. I most certainly have. Very witty. Of their kind, the very best there is. My father was an underrated, underappreciated artist. One day he'll be rediscovered. Perhaps his death will spark a revival. That would be the only fortunate consequence of his passing."

Damn it. I *was* starting to like this guy.

"I've even read one of *your* books," he said. "I liked it, rather. I can see why my father might be proud of his student."

"You said you envied me," I said, a little embarrassed by his flattery, "for being close to your father. I wasn't. He had a wall up he never quite let me get behind."

Jerome nodded. "I think that was true even of his wives—with the possible exception of Evelyn the Grotesque."

When he spoke her name he might have been sucking a lemon. I must've shown in my face my surprise at the depth of his bitterness, because he went on to answer a question I never asked.

"Evelyn stole my father from my mother. It's that simple. To me, she's a thief, and, in a roundabout way, a murderess. But she understood Roscoe Kane. She could relate to him on his own level—trade off-color, wise-guy cracks with him like a drag queen Gat Garson. And, of course, she drank with him. They were boozers together. That can create an enormous bond, you know. It's a club you can't resign from."

"He eventually left her."

Jerome shrugged. "They both went on the wagon. They both periodically fell off, in years to come; but for a while there, they were sober. It's a terrible thing to sober up and look at the person you've been married to when that person has simultaneously sobered up and is looking at the person she is married to, too. Neither one recognizes the sober version, and, well, the rest is history."

"And history is Mae Kane."

His smile turned up at both corners now. "Bless her greedy little heart. She was my mother's unintentional avenger. She was Evelyn's karma come home to roost. Those years of drinking turned pleasantly plump Evelyn into a barrel with legs, remember. And Mae was—and is—an attractive woman, to say the least. You've noticed?"

I rubbed my forehead. "I have noticed."

"Mae stole Evelyn away from my father, just as Evelyn had stolen him from my mother. My father always had a weakness for a bosomy babe, as Gat might say. Perhaps his lechery is what put me off the girls, that and being a momma's boy . . . the old cliché about being raised by your mommy, being your mommy's bestest friend, all of that was true in my case. Till she died."

"I, uh . . . never really heard the circumstances of your mother's death. Roscoe never got into it. That was one of the things he kept behind that wall I couldn't get back of."

"Guilt was back there, too," Jerome said. "Guilt's another thing he had back of that wall of his. He blamed himself. But I don't know that he was to blame, much. It was ten years after he left her that she killed herself."

"Jesus," I said. "I didn't know . . . I'm sorry . . ."

"Your condolences are noted, and appreciated," Jerome said, "if a few decades late. My mother, Winifred Kane, killed herself with a gun my father had given her to protect herself with. One of those Gat Garson guns he had half a dozen of."

I swallowed. "A long-barreled .38."

"Yes." Jerome smiled. "The kind my father posed with on his book covers."

I felt suddenly cold. "That's a piece of information I could've lived without."

"One might say the same for my mother. Oh, young lady?"

He stopped the barmaid for another Scotch and tonic. I asked for another Coke—but I had her put some bourbon in with it, this time.

"Jerome, I'm sorry to ask this . . ."

"Ask, ask."

"Why . . . why did your mother take her life? Did—did she leave a note . . .? What had been going on that—"

Jerome shrugged elaborately. "I was a teen-ager, all wrapped up in my own pubescent angst. I had little time to notice my mother's troubles. Oh, we were close. Very close. But she wore a mask, for me. A mother mask. The woman beneath was never fully revealed to me. What made her tick is a mystery even Gat Garson could not solve. I do know she had what might be euphemistically referred to as 'mental problems.' She was diagnosed schizophrenic, and was in and out of institutions where she had countless shock treatments, back while she and my father were married. My father admitted to me that his heavy drinking began in those days. And I can understand why the prospect of, shall we say, joining with the mentally stable Evelyn was an irresistible one. Besides, she had bigger titties than Mother."

The bitterness under the poised, Noel Coward exterior was cracking through. I'd known he was largely a pose; but I hadn't understood the nature of the pose. I hadn't guessed how sad and angry the real man, behind Jerome Kane's wall, really was.

I sipped the bourbon and Coke. Let the intense moment subside.

Then I said, "You saw your father last night."

He nodded. "For supper. We ate at an Italian place on the North Side, Augustino's, a favorite of his. Quite good. But, then, you saw him, too, didn't you? Right before he died? That's why I wanted to see you, Mallory. I wanted to ask you about that final meeting with him. . . ."

"I'll make you a deal. We'll get to my story after I hear yours."

"You tell me yours, I'll tell you mine? Why not. We're all brothers under the skin. I have seen my father rarely these past twenty years. He took me for a month each summer when I was growing up. But when I moved to San Francisco, after dropping out of college, and he began to get a sense of . . . my lifestyle . . . our contact became, well, infrequent."

"Roscoe never could accept that you're gay, could he?"

Jerome nodded, looking into the smoky-colored drink. "Quite right. Why, exactly, I couldn't tell you. Perhaps he saw it as a rejection of him. Gat Garson

116

was an idealized version of himself, you know—oh, Gat was a put-on, a spoof, but still . . . Gat *was* macho, and in not a wholly satirical way. Gat Garson was a genuine tough guy, just like Mike Hammer or James Bond. And my father was macho himself, a brawler, particularly in the verbal sense. And, like Gat, he was a womanizer. He loved those blondes with the big boobies—or he did in the early days. I've sensed, the few times I was with him in recent years, a declining interest in honey-haired darlings, his lechery fading to but a passing mammary. Speaking of which—miss?"

He asked for a third Scotch and tonic; I kept nibbling at my bourbon and Coke.

Then he went on. "Anyway, my father may have looked upon my life-style as a conscious rejection of everything he stood for, as a man. And of course it wasn't." He laughed, raucously. "It was a *subconscious* rejection." He laughed again, but softly. "I did feel a conscious bitterness about my mother's death. I did blame him, at least partially. But I didn't want him out of my life. He was the only parent I had left. I would've liked for him to accept me. That, I would've liked very much."

The third Scotch and tonic came, and he started right in on it.

I said, "I think your father was proud of what you've achieved."

He raised an eyebrow. "Possibly you're right. I sensed, or hoped I sensed, he was pleased with what I'd accomplished, proud of my fashion designs being shown in major cities here and in Europe, of my name having gained a certain recognizability of its own, of my financial success, *especially* my financial success. For a Depression child like Roscoe Kane, money is the major measure."

"You probably got your artistic bent from him."

"No doubt," he said. "I didn't get it from my mother. She had few talents—just her good looks, which started to go on her when her mental problems took hold. But we've been down that path before; let's go elsewhere."

"What did you and your father talk about?"

"Last night, you mean? We . . . we made ammends, you might say. I can't go so far as to say he came right out and accepted me for what I am—admitted he knew I was gay and that he could accept me as such. But he did say something that approximated that; well, two things, actually."

"What were they?"

He smiled on one side of his face. "First"—and he imitated his father's gruff voice, to perfection—"Jerome, sex is overrated."

I smiled. "What was the other thing?"

Jerome shrugged, looked in the drink. "Just that it was nice to have a son."

I sat and looked into my bourbon and Coke and pretended not to notice him wipe the tear from beneath one china-blue eye.

"He was chatting with Cynthia Crystal," he said, "when I left him in the lobby around nine-thirty. That was the last time I saw him."

"Cynthia Crystal?"

"Yes—the author."

"I know her. How do you know her, Jerome?"

"I don't—I recognized her from a talk show. Fine writer."

"Yes, she is."

"Oddly—when I glanced back, their conversation seemed to have heated up."

"Really? Were they arguing?"

He thought about that. "I wouldn't go that far. 'Having words' is more like it."

"How did your father happen to know Cynthia?"

He shrugged, draining the Scotch and tonic. "I don't know that he did."

This morning, when I'd spoken to Cynthia, she hadn't mentioned speaking to Roscoe Kane. From the detached way she'd referred to him, I'd assumed she'd never met the man.

"I know why I envy you," Jerome said suddenly, softly.

"Why?"

"Not because you were close to him. Nobody, except perhaps Evelyn the Grotesque, was close to him. And then only when they were in their cups. . . ."

Silence.

Then he said: "You were the son he always wanted me to be."

I tried to bridge the awkwardness gap. "Look—it wasn't that way . . . I was just a fan."

"No. Much more than that. You were a surrogate son. And you had access to him in a way I never did. You pleased him in ways I never could. And I envy you that. I resent you for that."

There wasn't anything to say, so I didn't.

He said, "Now. We had a bargain. You're to tell me about you and my father, last night."

"Why, are you suspicious?"

He blinked. "Suspicious?"

"About the circumstances surrounding his death. Is that why you're asking questions?"

"I don't know what you're talking about," he said ingenuously. "I just want to know what my father said."

"What he said?"

119

He leaned across the table and looked at me with his father's eyes and the earnestness and trembling lower lip of a child. "About me. Did he mention me? Did he say anything about me?"

I was one of the last to see his father alive; he wanted to know if he'd been in his father's thoughts. . . .

So I told him Roscoe had mentioned what a wonderful evening he'd had with him, that it was obvious he thought the world of Jerome.

And Jerome sighed, and said thank you, told me I could reach him at Troy's till he left for the Milwaukee services Monday, and left.

I just sat there for a while, shaking my head.

Then just as I'd gotten up to go, a hand settled on my shoulder and I glanced back.

"Let's talk, asshole."

And I punched Gregg Gorman in the stomach.

11

I DON'T make a practice of punching people in the stomach, or anywhere else for that matter. Even the likes of Gregg Gorman. I was immediately embarrassed and sorry—even if the feel of my fist sinking into his beer belly had been satisfying, in a mindless, macho, Gat Garson sort of way.

He didn't go down or anything; he just doubled over. Nobody except that table of Sardini, Christian and a few others had seen it. So the management didn't come rushing over and throw me out the door on my butt. Nor did a John Wayne-type table-and-chair-smashing brawl break out. Gorman wasn't the type to retaliate, except verbally—or with a two-by-four while you were asleep.

He held his stomach and breathed hard and then pretended to be hurt worse than he was. The beady eyes under the bushy eyebrows were full of dollar signs as he said, "I'm gonna sue you, Mallory, you little creep."

"Shouldn't you call the cops first, and get me charged with assault and battery?"

"Maybe I'll do that. Maybe I will."

"Better round up your witnesses."

He glanced over at the table where Sardini and crew sat, smiling, talking, back in their own conversation. "They're friends of yours," he said.

"That's true."

"Maybe we should just step outside," he said, puffing himself up like a squat little bear, "and finish this ..." And there was a blank space where his favorite term of endearment for me would've gone, had he had the nerve to use it again.

I nodded toward the door. "There's an alley behind the hotel."

He rubbed a hand over his face; indeterminate flecks drifted down from his goatee—dandruff, food, whatever.

And then he sat down at the table.

I stood looking at him.

He looked up and got a completely false smile going and said, "Maybe I deserved that punch in the belly. Maybe I shouldn't've called you that. And maybe I screwed you that time, a little, where your pal Wheeler was concerned. So I'm willing to forgive and forget this little incident. Come on, Mallory—sit down."

I sat. But I didn't forgive, or forget.

"You said you wanted to talk," I said. I wanted to talk to him, too. But I'd let him go first. . . .

He shrugged, elaborately. "I just wanted to straighten you out on some shit."

Classy guy; a publishing magnate with a real way with words. He used to own used-car lots, and had reportedly made a fortune or two before he somewhat self-indulgently turned to the pursuit of publishing in the mystery field, having been a fan since his teens. I bought his books, but I wouldn't buy a used car from him.

"What is it you want to straighten me out on, Gorman?"

"Call me Gregg. And I'll call you . . ."

"Asshole?"

He pushed the air with two palms, in a peace-making gesture I didn't believe for a split second.

"Let's put that behind us," he said, with his used-car dealer's smile.

"Let's. What do you want to straighten me out on, Gregg?"

"I cleaned up my act, Mallory," he said. "Changed my image."

If not his underwear.

"Look, I admit I pulled some . . . shady deals, from time to time. I'm a little guy. I gotta look after myself. You gotta give me credit for some good work—I got some stuff back in print that you like seein' back in print, right?"

I admitted as much.

"I'm just a one-man show," he said, "tryin' to keep my little boat afloat. The mystery fan market isn't any vast audience by a long shot—and you know it, or you'd dress better."

Look who was talking.

"It's a small market," I said, "but you publish expensive books. On that slipcased set of Carroll John Daly's Race Williams novels you had several thousand sales—chickenfeed for a mass-market publisher, but for a specialty guy like you? At two hundred bucks a set? You're making a killing."

He shrugged, less elaborately this time. "I couldn't afford to publish nice books when I was starting out. And you know the quality of the stuff I do—the printing, the binding, the paper, all that crap, is top of the line."

That was true: his books were every bit as attractive as he wasn't.

"But Gregg, old buddy," I said, "you're not doing anybody any *favors*, turning out fancy expensive books. You may be providing a service of sorts, to mystery fans who're into this stuff, but if you weren't turning out high-quality merchandise, you couldn't charge the high prices. So don't bother bragging to me. It doesn't cut you any slack, where I'm concerned."

He waved a waitress over and asked for two beers (both for himself).

He said, "All I'm getting at is I wasn't able to start out doing fancy schmancy books. I did these sorta oversize, trade-type paperbacks, remember?"

"I remember. The Raoul Wheeler books were paperbacks. You sold five thousand of each of those at eight bucks per and paid no royalties at all. You had a free ride on a guy dying of cancer. Brag about *that*."

Gorman shrugged again. "I'm not proud of it," he allowed. "By the way, I'm bringing those Wheelers back out again, hardback this time. You wanna do those intros we talked about way back when? With a credit on the covers? I'll pay you. Make it up to you."

"You'll do me that little favor, now that I've published some books and have a name for myself. You're a peach, Gorman."

The beers came; Gorman put one away in a couple of chugs, then sipped at the other as he said, "I been tryin' to make a point, but you won't let me. I been tryin' to say that a few shady-type deals I pulled, early on, that I'm not proud of having done, is what got me capitalized to the point where I could put together a little publishing company that's giving mystery fans beautiful books. My Daly set won a special award from the Mystery Writers of America, y'know. An Edgar Allan Poe award. You ever win an Edgar, Mallory?"

"No," I said. "But then my philosophy isn't the Edgar justifies the means."

"Eat your heart out, schmuck," he said, grinning over the lip of the beer; foam rode the edge of his mustache.

"Wipe your face, Gorman," I said, "before I wipe it for you."

He snorted. "You read too many Gat Garson books, Mallory. Speaking of which . . . you oughta be grateful I'm bringing your idol's books out, instead of givin' me a bad time over it."

So that was what this was about.

"Oh," I said, "you didn't like my comment about how Roscoe's books'll be more valuable to you, with him dead."

"That's a lousy thing to say. And not necessarily true. The few thousand extra copies we'll sell, of each of 'em, is hardly grounds for . . ." He searched for the word in his beer; he didn't find it.

So I gave it to him: "Murder?"

He looked up sharply. "Is that what you think, Mallory?"

"Is what what I think?"

"That Roscoe was . . . killed, or something."

"What if it is?"

"I heard you . . . were up there, when . . ." He drank a little beer. Then: "I heard you found the body."

It was getting around, finally.

"Maybe," I said.

"So, uh . . . what do you think? Was it murder?"

"Why do you care? What's your interest in Roscoe?"

"He was a friend. He was a buddy! I liked him."

"You like money."

"I like money, and I like people, too. Like Roscoe, I liked. Hell, I even like you, Mallory."

"And you're heartsick about Roscoe's death."

He shook his head sadly, side to side. "Tragic loss to the mystery community."

"Jesus, Gorman, you ought to volunteer to do his eulogy. You'd have to wear a clean sweater, though."

"Just don't . . . don't go implying what you implied before, in public, or maybe . . . maybe I *will* sue you."

"What are you talking about?"

"Implying I . . . that's stupid. I loved Roscoe."

"You used to just like him. Do you love *me* now, or is it still just 'like'?"

"Screw you."

"Must be love. Tell you what. I won't accuse you publicly of murdering Roscoe; I won't even imply it. Unless, of course, I find out you did it."

He got huffily self-righteous. "Don't be stupid. What motive would I have for that? To make the books of his I'm publishing sell a little better? Nobody'd kill anybody over that."

"Where were you?"

"Where . . . where was I when?"

"When Roscoe was murdered."

He swallowed. The red nose seemed to throb in the near-darkness. "You really *do* think it was murder."

"I really do."

"Have you told the cops?"

"I've tried."

"Yeah, and?"

"And they don't seem to be paying much attention. Yet."

He smirked and waved for the waitress. "You don't *know* that it was murder," he said. "It *could've* been accidental."

"Could've been," I granted. "Like when Nixon's secretary accidentally erased the tape."

126

"I think you should leave this alone."

"I think you should answer my question."

"What question?"

"Where were you last night? When Roscoe was dying in the tub?"

The beers came, but he didn't dig in; he sat looking at them and summoned a look of confidence up and tried it out on me. I didn't think much of it. It accompanied the following declaration: "I was with my angels."

Gorman being with anybody's angels, let alone his own, was a little hard to picture.

"Your angels," I said.

"Yeah, you know. My angels. My backers. The guys that invest in me. The guys that sign the checks."

It was coming back to me now; I'd heard about this, from somebody—Sardini, I thought. Seemed Gorman's financial backing, his working capital— that is to say, the working capital he didn't generate himself, swindling innocents like me and old-timers like Raoul Wheeler—came from a pair of Chicago-area longtime mystery fans, guys in their forties who were partners in a chain of bookstores. Those bookstores were the kind with the windows painted out and lots of Xs on the front.

Pornographers is what Gorman's angels were.

Or at least, pornography merchants. In bed with the mob, so rumor said; which made Gorman vaguely mob-dirty, too.

"You were with your angels," I said.

"Yeah, having dinner at the Berghoff."

The Berghoff was a popular German restaurant in downtown Chicago, and had been since the late Mayor Daley was in diapers.

"So a lot of people saw you," I said.

He smiled. "A lot of people saw us."

127

"Conveniently saw you."

"No, damn it, just *saw* us! Leave it alone, Mallory. Leave it alone."

"Or?"

"Did I say 'or'? I don't remember saying 'or.' Just friendly advice from your favorite publisher: leave it alone."

"I'd like to talk to your angels."

"Stay away from them, for your own good. They're nice guys, but they're not as nice as me. And come to think of it, stay away from me. Quit smart-mouthing me. And stay away from Kathy Wickman, too, while you're at it."

"Or?"

He nodded, a yellow smile peeking out of the brush of his goatee. "Yeah. *Or.*"

"Tell me something, Gorman. Your little company's been doing pretty good; you've won an Edgar, you're making good dough, you're getting some of your titles into the major bookstore chains. This unpublished Hammett novel you discovered, tell me. Why aren't you publishing it yourself? Why'd you lay it off on a major publisher, when you could've made the big score yourself?"

His face, with the exception of the goatee and the reddish nose, went white.

And he got up and waddled out without another word, leaving his two beers behind.

12

I STEPPED out into the chilly afternoon, zipping my light jacket. Rain spit in my face. It was a lousy afternoon to go sightseeing. Nevertheless, I got on the old bus—a former Greyhound with the words "Crime Tour" in the destination slot over the front windows—and joined a couple dozen other hearty souls, among them (halfway back) Kathy Wickman, who smiled with surprise when she saw me, patting the seat next to her. I sat down.

"Thought you said you weren't going to take this particular ride," Kathy said, with yet another wry smile.

"Maybe I couldn't wait till supper to see you again."

"I'm flattered. But why so intense?"

"Huh?"

"You have a furrow in your brow deep enough to hide a dime in."

"Hey—that's a Roscoe Kane line."

She nodded. "I know. I bought myself a copy of *The Dame Dealt Death* in the dealers' room, from a woman dealer, appropriately enough. Read the first couple of chapters when I was relaxing before coming down to catch this bus."

"And?"

"Kind of liked what I read. Fun, in a dated way."

"Chandler seems dated, too, you know."

"I wouldn't agree, but I do admit seeing more merit in Kane than I would ever have guessed. I'll have fun reading it."

"Glad to see you have an open mind."

Up at the front of the bus, Cynthia Crystal was getting on. She nodded and smiled at the tall, lanky, Zappa-bearded driver/guide. She still wore the gray slacks outfit; despite a long day of dealing with fans and such, she looked bandbox fresh. Tim Culver was not with her.

"I *do* have an open mind," Kathy said, "but not so open that I don't find it less than flattering when your attention shifts to some other female."

"Well, Cynthia's an old friend."

"Your brow's furrowed again."

"Kathy, Cynthia's why I'm here. I need to talk to her. I called her room and was told she was going to take the Crime Tour."

Told in rather clipped words by Tim Culver, actually.

"Mal," Kathy said, wry as ever, "I'm hurt, naturally—but I'll be over it by supper."

I smiled again, nodded and got up, walked up the aisle and sat next to Cynthia.

"Why, Mal," she said, her short pale-blond hair swinging as she turned her head. "How nice. I was hoping we might have a few moments alone this weekend."

The bus began moving.

I laughed, just a little. "On a bus with twenty or thirty other people, you mean?"

"Without Tim around, I mean."

"How long have you two been, uh—"

130

"An item? A year and a half. Living together? Six months."

"I envy him."

"It may not last." She said this coolly, with seeming lack of interest. She might have been talking about the weather, or the latest fad in women's shoes.

But behind Cynthia Crystal's brittle façade was a woman as sensitive as she was intelligent. In her light blue eyes, her hurt was showing.

"What's the problem with you and Tim? If you don't mind my asking."

"Jealousy. Pure and simple. Even if he doesn't know it."

"Jealousy? My stopping by at your table this morning didn't set this off, did it? Didn't you explain to Tim that we never amounted to anything?"

"Speak for yourself, darling," she said, twisting my meaning for the fun of it. "I've amounted to something. That's the problem."

"What do you mean?"

She sighed. "It's not jealousy of the green-eyed variety, not unless that green is money-shade. Tim's jealous of my success—particularly my monetary success. My last novel—as well as the Hammett biography—sold more copies than all the sales of all his books combined."

Over the slightly static-ridden intercom, the tour guide was speaking. "Welcome to the Hagenauer Chicago Crime Tour, ladies and gentlemen. Unfortunately, many of Chicago's most famous—and infamous—buildings have made way for urban renewal and/or blight. The Hotel Metropole, where Al Capone held court, and Big Jim Colosimo's Four Deuces, a nightclub where you might see George M. Cohan or Enrico Caruso sitting at the next table, are today a vacant lot and a parking lot, respectively. The 'toughest red-light district west of the Barbary Coast,' the notorious Levee is, alas, just a memory—there's a housing project where the most elaborate sporting house of 'em all, the Everleigh Club, once stood. Rather than visit these pale shadows, we'll head to the near North Side, and along the way I'll be pointing out some of the Chicago criminal landmarks that are still standing."

We were on State Street now, going north, moving slow behind a CTA bus. Cynthia was looking out her window at the sidewalks jammed with people, and the big department stores, whose windows were already looking Christmas-y.

We sat silently for a while. Then, without looking at me, she said reflectively, "I don't mean to make Tim sound petty or venal. He's neither. It's just"— and now she looked at me—"he's had this situation with his brother, Curt, where Curt got all the breaks, at least where financial success is concerned."

"But Tim's gotten the glory."

She shrugged. "He's had some critical success. But his following is basically cult. And, as Tim is known to say, 'The definition of a cult is seven readers short of a writer's being able to make a living.' "

We rode in silence; the next person to speak was our driver/tour guide, over his squawky intercom: "This is the site of Terrible Tommy's bust-out."

He was referring to a six-story building of rough-hewn stone up ahead; the side of the building we were looking at was latticed with fire escapes.

"Used as an administration building today," he said, slowing down (the bus, not his speech), "the structure on our right, its stone cut from quarried rock, was then the Criminal Courts Building from which Terrible Tommy—a murderer sentenced to hang by the neck till dead—escaped, running across

132

the adjacent prison yard where that modern firehouse, there, now stands. The authorities have been required, by the original court order, to hold the gallows constructed for Terrible Tommy's departure until the lad is apprehended. It's still stored in the basement of that very building."

We were looking out the window back at it, now.

The driver continued: "Since Terrible Tommy escaped in 1921, and Tommy would be in his nineties today, the gallows is unlikely to be used."

Pretty soon we were back on State Street, heading toward our next bloody landmark.

"I didn't know you went in for this kind of thing," I told her.

She tossed off the facial equivalent of an elegant little shrug. "I'm a true crime buff of sorts, like any mystery writer. Chicago is the Disneyland of crime, after all; gotta see the sights."

"I also didn't know you knew Roscoe Kane."

She was looking out the window; her face tensed, barely, but she didn't look back at me. "I didn't, really."

"His son, Jerome, said you and Roscoe spoke in the lobby last night. Not long before Roscoe's death."

"That's true."

"Why didn't you mention it this morning?"

She looked at me, the cool blue of her eyes turning cooler. "And here I thought you sidling up and sitting down next to me was social. I was feeling downright girlish."

"I thought this morning we decided we were friends. The time I tried to be more than a friend to you was sort of a disaster, as you'll recall."

"I'm just not interested in one-night stands. I never said it was *impossible* for me to do more than like you, Mal."

"That's nice to hear."

"At the moment, however, I don't know if I even like you anymore. I begin to feel a little used."

"That's unfair. You went out of your way not to mention having seen Roscoe when we spoke this morning. Why?"

"That's simply not the case, Mal. I just didn't think to mention it."

The intercom interrupted. "That parking lot to your left is the site of Dion O'Banion's flower shop—where Al Capone's minions shot the florist/gangster amid his own roses on November 10, 1924. Across the street is Holy Name Cathedral—take a close look and you may still be able to make out where machine-gun bullets kissed the side of the building; Al Capone's men, again, and they weren't trying to kiss the Pope's ring by proxy—those kisses were thrown at Hymie Weiss, who caught 'em. October 11, 1926."

Cynthia spoke, her mouth pursed with irony. "Our tour guide sounds as if your mentor Roscoe Kane wrote his patter."

"It is colorful, at that. What about Roscoe, Cynthia? How did you know him?"

She looked at me sharply. "I *didn't*, Mal. I recognized him in the lobby, from his bookjacket photos. And I spoke to him, introduced myself. And we chatted. That's all."

"What did you chat about?"

"Small talk. Nothing."

"Jerome said your conversation heated up. You argued."

She looked out the window again. "We didn't argue."

"Jerome misread the situation, then."

"Yes."

"What did you chat about, Cynthia?"

134

She looked at me again. "Really, Mal, I'm losing patience with you—not to mention any remaining semblance of affection I might have had. Why is my personal conversation with Roscoe Kane of any interest to you?"

"Because I think Roscoe may have been murdered."

That startled her, but just momentarily. Then, of all things, she laughed—just a little. Cocktail-party laugh.

I said, "What the hell's funny about that?"

"Just the idea of life imitating fiction. The notion of somebody walking around playing amateur detective, like a character in a silly novel."

"Like the characters in your silly novels, you mean."

"Actually, I was thinking more along the lines of the characters in *your* silly novels, dear. Now, why don't you go back and sit by the little brunette one-night stand who's been watching us? She looks lonely."

"What did you and Roscoe Kane talk about?"

"I simply introduced myself to him, told him I'd enjoyed his books, and he bit my head off, the unpleasant little bastard."

"Why'd he bite your head off?"

"I'd said something deprecatory about him, in passing, in my Hammett book. Mentioned him as 'one of the lesser lights' of the original *Black Mask* crowd. He took offense."

That sounded like Roscoe.

"That was it, then?"

"That was it," she said, terse as a telegram.

"Why didn't you just tell me this in the first place?"

"What business was it of yours?"

She had a point.

"I'm sorry if I've been rude," I told her. "I thought we were friends. I didn't think you'd mind my . . ."

"Treating me like a suspect in a Perry Mason story? Why, I love it. It's more fun than playing strip *Clue*. Now, go away. You disappoint me."

I got up, stepped out into the aisle; Cynthia reached a hand out and touched my arm.

"Mal—forgive me. I know what Roscoe meant to you. I don't mean to make light of that, or of your need to . . . ask some questions, in the wake of his death."

"It's okay, Cynthia. I can understand your attitude."

"No, I don't think you do. I'm having a rocky time of it with Tim—this weekend was supposed to be a getaway for us, a place, a time, for us to patch up our problems. But all we've done is bicker. And the mood I'm in just spilled over onto you a bit. Forgive me."

"No forgiveness needed."

"Maybe I'm just regretting shooing you away, at that Bouchercon, once upon a time."

I smiled. "I know *I* still regret that."

"You would. Now, shoo. Go sit with your little brunette in her sweatshirt."

"She's the editor of *Noir*, you know, not some teenager I picked up."

"Isn't that sweet," she said. As usual, her malice was tempered with good humor. She could be bitchy, my Cynthia, but never a bitch.

Pretty soon I was sitting next to Kathy, and the bus was tooling along Lincoln Avenue. Our driver pointed out the site of John Dillinger's death, the Biograph Theater—after all these years, still a study in '30s art-deco black and white, though Bergman's *Fanny and Alexander* was playing there, not *Manhattan Melodrama*. Then a few minutes later we were shown the site of the garage where the St. Valentine's Day Massacre had taken place, on the west side of Clark Street.

"Those two white pillars are all that remain of S-M-C Cartage Company," he said. A modern housing center for the elderly, set back from the street, was where the garage once had been.

Before long, the bus rumbled over a massive drawbridge, its huge metal shoulders looming, and the driver said, "On our left is the La Salle-Wacker building, where mayor Anton Cermak's personal police bodyguards, Miller and Lang, attempted the assassination of Frank Nitti in December 1932. The attempt failed, but within weeks, Mayor Cermak himself fell under an assassin's gun."

We drove down the concrete canyon of La Salle Street—the driver pointed out the looming city hall at the left, calling it, "The scene of many a Chicago crime"—and dead-ended at the gigantic art-deco Board of Trade Building. Whether or not it, too, was a crime site, the driver didn't say.

"Well," Kathy said, as the bus turned left, on its way back to the Congress, "I guess we've seen Chicago, all right."

"Not quite."

"Oh?"

"Not till you've had the deep-dish pizza."

We smiled at each other, and held hands like kids in love; once Cynthia glanced back at us.

She seemed vaguely sad.

13

GINO'S on Rush Street was half a flight down off the sidewalk. Once inside, low-ceilinged interconnecting rooms went on forever, rooms whose walls were lined with graffiti and graffiti-carved wooden booths, and so full of people that the place managed to seem simultaneously claustrophobic and sprawling. And also bustling, this Friday night. The smell of tomato sauce in the air was so rich you could gain weight breathing, and it was intermingled with cigarette smoke so thick you could also get a side dish of emphysema. Gino's was one of half a dozen places in Chicago that claimed to be the originator of Chicago-style, deep-dish pizza; I didn't know if their claim was the legitimate one or not, but I did know that I hadn't made a visit to Chicago in the last twenty years without stopping in to sample the evidence.

This was Kathy Wickman's first time at Gino's. In gray slacks and a pink Norma Kamali top with padded shoulders, she had a '40s look appropriate to her position as editor of a magazine called *Noir*—and for the era when Gino's had apparently last been redecorated. I guided her by the arm to the narrow main aisle, where I then had to ease her out in front of me, as side-by-side passage was out of the question. We had our work cut out for us, trailing a red-haired, harried, red-aproned middle-aged waitress who went barreling down the labyrinth, and Kathy glanced back with wide eyes and a frenzied smile that questioned my sanity in bringing her here.

Finally we were in a little booth, facing each other, and she glanced at the carvings in the wall next to her—saying, among other things, *ComicCon '84*, *Spock Lives* and *Ed loves Carol*—and said, "So this is your idea of 'atmosphere'?"

"It's a question of semantics."

With a good-natured smirk, she said, "It's a question of building code, is more like it."

"Hey, this place *is* Chicago. Fast and obnoxious and fattening. Also, fun."

"I thought you didn't like big cities."

"I like big cities fine. I even like New York. But I also like pretending I don't when New Yorkers are around."

"Still, you obviously like Chicago better than New York City."

"That's probably only because I know Chicago better. I've been coming in here once or twice a year since I was a high-school kid. My kind of town."

"You and Sinatra. And this is your kind of town's kind of place, huh. What else do you do in the big city for fun?"

"I'll show you. We'll take a tour that'll beat that Crime bus all silly. We'll take a cab down to Old Town, after we eat, and walk around and end up at Second City."

Her face lit up. "Don't you need reservations way in advance for that?"

"I know a guy in the cast; called him this afternoon and he got us in."

"That's great! I always wanted to see Second City."

"It's always a good show—they practically invented improv' comedy. I've followed 'em for years."

"You're spoiling your small-town image for me, Mal."

"Really? I was hoping my books didn't project the typical small-town image—you know, the notion that Iowa was one big cornfield and a general store with a couple old guys playing checkers and chewing tobacco out front."

She smiled with her eyes. "I think your novels do, to an extent, knock down that stereotype. But the small-town ambiance comes through. . . ."

"Ambiance. Is that French?"

"Okay, okay—so I'm a pretentious little magazine editor . . . and don't ask whether it's me or the magazine that's little, okay? But reading a story set in Port City, Iowa, is different than reading a story set in New York or L.A. or Chicago. Like John D. MacDonald doing Florida. So do me a favor and promise not to do any stories set in a big city; stick with your small-town settings."

"I promise," I said.

The waitress returned for our order and I asked for a small pepperoni and a couple of Italian salads and a couple of beers.

"Anyway," Kathy said, "I guess your fair-to-middling Chicago savvy is supposed to fool me into accepting this basement as a restaurant, and these subway walls as atmosphere."

"Are you really put off by this place?"

Wry grin #459. "Not at all. I love it, actually. It's just not my idea of atmosphere. I think the word is more like . . . ambiance."

Our beers arrived just in time for us to toast the joint.

"Spoken like a true editor of *Noir* magazine," I said.

Her expression shifted; the shadow of the wry smile remained, but she was suddenly, vaguely, somber.

"I ran into my publisher," she said, "when I was on my way down to meet you in the lobby, for dinner."

"I ran into him, too. I punched him in the stomach, actually."

She nearly did a spit-take; she said, "No fooling?"

"Hey, I'm not proud of it, really. I don't go around punching people."

Revving up the wry smile again, she said, "Why not? Gat Garson did."

"Gat Garson's a fun character in a book. But a less than sterling role model."

"What happened between you and Gregg, anyway?"

"We just did some name calling, followed by an attempt to bury the hatchet—in each other's heads. The usual. What was your conversation with him like?"

She paused, then said, "He stopped me in the hall and invited me up to a cocktail party in his room tonight."

"When?"

"The 'con's showing the first movie version of *The Maltese Falcon* at midnight, the 1931 version with Ricardo Cortez, and Gregg's never seen it, so he's rounding some people up to go and then after go back to his room for expensive nightcaps."

"You're sure you're not the only one invited?"

She laughed, a little. "Gregg doesn't have the courage to come on to me, not overtly. He likes to play little games. He's into a more paternal trip, actually."

"That'd make it incest."

"No, really. Those little passes he makes, if I took him up on one of 'em, he'd fold up like a folding chair. He's married, you know—his wife's ill and he treats her like a princess. His one redeeming trait, it would seem. I'd also guess he's faithful to her."

"Doesn't sound like the Gregg Gorman I know and love to hate."

"Nobody's perfect, Mal, and nobody's perfectly rotten, either. Even Gregg. Of course, I could be wrong about his being a faithful hubby. Still, I don't think he'd fool with me; I'm too valuable to him—*Noir*'s a feather in his cap, and, not to sound *too* very egotistical, I am *Noir*. And, as Gregg might say, you don't defecate where you dine."

"That's not *exactly* how he'd put it."

"True. But, shit, I'm much more elegant than Gregg."

This time *I* smiled wryly, and we toasted beer glasses again.

"He also warned me," she said guardedly, "about hanging out with you. He said he'd prefer it if I didn't."

"Is that how he put it?"

"Not exactly. That's the elegant version. But he says you're just using me."

"I'd kind of like to, at that."

"Let's not get ahead of ourselves, now, Mal. Here are our salads."

We began eating, and I said, "What did he mean by that, exactly?"

"What?"

"What did he mean, I'm 'using' you?"

"Oh! To get at him."

"To get at him, how?"

"He said you're trying to pin something on him. That's all he said." She shrugged and returned to her salad.

"He means Roscoe's murder," I said.

142

She looked up from her salad, gave me a sharp, stunned look. "Murder?"

I sighed and poked at my salad. "Yeah. Murder."

And I told her about it.

"Hell!" she said. "You're playing detective, aren't you? Just like your books . . ."

"Oh, please, don't start."

"What do you mean?"

"Everybody and his duck thinks I'm poking around Roscoe's death looking for a book to write. That isn't it at all."

"What is it, then?"

"Come on, Kathy—Roscoe Kane was my friend. He was . . . more than that. He was . . . well, as other people have put it . . . my mentor."

"He was your hero."

"Yeah. He was my hero."

"And a man's gotta do what a man's gotta do."

"Bullshit. If the assistant coroner would've listened to me, and brought the cops in, I'd've done a fast fade by now. You think murder's my idea of a good time? God!"

Eyeing me with poorly hidden suspicion, fork in her salad jabbing at the side of the bowl, missing the few remaining shreds of lettuce entirely, she said, "*Are* you using me? Or planning to use me, to spy on Gorman or something?"

"It hadn't even occurred to me."

"Good."

"Though it isn't a bad idea."

She smiled in spite of herself; one of her rare open-mouth smiles that showed a little too much gum, like Norma Jean Baker before she and Hollywood conspired to invent Marilyn Monroe.

"You," she said, "are incorrigible."

I shrugged. "Then don't incorrige me."

143

She smiled some more, but her smile was back to its usual wry-pixie self, and she shook her head and pushed her now-empty salad bowl aside. She said, "If you want some help, I might give it to you."

"I'll give it some thought. If I think of something worthwhile, I might ask."

"I might answer. But you got to promise me something . . ."

"Okay."

"Promise me you won't turn this into a book."

"All right."

The pizza came, steaming hot and smelling very, very good. Kathy'd never had Chicago-style pizza before—except the pale shadow of a Pizza Hut variety—and she was an instant convert. Saucy, cheesy, with a pastrylike sweet crust, Gino's pizza was an Italian-American atonement for the Mafia.

And nearly as fatal: one small pizza had stuffed us both and we sat and sipped a second beer, each sip painful.

"I never ate so much in my life," Kathy said.

"You'll be over it in a week," I said. "Kathy, is something bothering you besides a full stomach?"

She sighed, nodded; said, "You don't, uh . . . really suspect Gregg of . . ." She couldn't say it.

I smiled. "The editor of a magazine devoted to fictional crime and violence, and you can't say that simple word found in so many titles of the books you review: murder."

She shivered. "Fantasy's one thing . . . this is quite apart. Very disturbing."

"Finding Roscoe's body was no picnic, either."

"Do you? Suspect Gregg, I mean?"

"I suspect him of something. Not murder—not yet, anyway."

"What *do* you suspect him of?"

144

"Fraud."

"How so?"

"The Hammett book. I think it's a hoax."

"You can't be serious. . . ."

"Dead. I think it was ghosted. Probably very cleverly, very well-ghosted. But ghosted."

"Who *by*, for heaven's sake?"

"There's a couple of possibilities. Tim Culver's the obvious suspect—he's the modern 'prime proponent' of the Hammett style. His live-in-lady, Cynthia Crystal, had access to the Hammett papers—maybe including other fragments that might've proved useful. Also, Cynthia's a fine writer, with respect for Hammett's work—her work bears his influence, in a way. She's a candidate for ghost herself. Or her and Culver together . . ."

"So you think one, or both, of them—"

"No. I think it was somebody else."

"*Who?*"

"Who do you think I'd think it'd be?"

She thought. "You can't be serious!"

"You said that before."

"Surely you don't suspect . . ."

"I surely do," I said. "I think Roscoe Kane ghosted *The Secret Emperor* by Dashiell Hammett."

She kept shaking her head, finding this harder to swallow than another bite of Gino's pizza. "But—was Kane a good enough writer to mimic *Hammett*, of all people, *and* get away with it?"

I nodded. "Yes. Few people know that, but yes, he was. He was that good a writer."

"And you think this had something to do with why Roscoe was. . ."

"Killed. Most likely. This is a big scam, Kathy. Hundreds of thousands of dollars involved, at the minimum."

145

The waitress brought our check.

Kathy looked at me almost mockingly, wagging her head; the long brown hair moved in waves. "But you don't know this for a fact. It may very well be an authentic unpublished Hammett novel; if it's a fake, it's fooled all the experts who've come in contact with it."

"So did the Hitler diaries, till the right experts came along."

She looked at me thoughtfully. "Think you could tell the difference, if you got hold of a copy?"

"I might be one of the few people familiar enough with both Roscoe Kane's work *and* Hammett's to nail it down, yes. Why?"

She shrugged facially. "Just wondering. Shall we go? Old Town's not getting any younger, you know."

"True," I admitted. I left the money on the table and we rose from the booth and slowly, weighted down by the pizza, made our way through the catacombs of Gino's and up the stairs and onto Rush Street.

"We'll catch a cab down at the corner," I said, putting my arm around her shoulder. The evening was chilly, but the neons of Rush Street seemed to warm it. Chicago was a terrific place.

A hand squeezed round my arm and it wasn't Kathy's.

I looked back and saw a burly guy about forty in a blue quilted jacket, a guy who looked like he'd been hit in the face long ago with a bag of nickels and had healed improperly; he was smiling at me with false, white teeth. He had a gray, balding butch that looked like a dying lawn; his eyes were a similar gray and deader-looking than his hair.

And he was hurting my arm.

"What do you want?" I said, trying to sound angry rather than scared.

He didn't say anything; he just proceeded to drag me along with him.

Kathy, speechless, was rushing along after us.

Before I could think of anything clever to say or bold to do, the guy had dragged me across traffic into the alley opposite, where two more guys waited. One of them, a stocky guy in a cowhide jacket, had hippie-length hair, only a love child he wasn't; the other, a much younger guy in an AC/DC sweatshirt, with pimples on his neck and shorter long hair, grabbed Kathy. Just a few feet inside the mouth of the alley, against the wall, he held a hand over her mouth and put an arm around her waist and she kicked and struggled but it didn't do her much good. A few yards away, people strolled by on the sidewalk, not noticing the fun and games in the dark alley nearby. Many were nibbling chocolate chip cookies purchased at the Mrs. Field's Cookies shop next to the alleyway.

As for me, I was about to toss mine. I was in the process of getting thrown against a brick wall and having a fist buried in my stomach by the guy who'd dragged me here, a couple of seconds, a couple of lifetimes, ago. I fell to my knees and, like they say at Gino's, one Chicago-style pizza, coming right up.

"Go back to the farm, smart-ass," said the guy who'd hit me. He had a voice as harsh as the gravel my hands were touching. I grabbed up a handful and tossed it at him and he went blind, for just a moment— long enough for me to throw a fist up into his groin and double him over.

And I got up on my feet and hit him on the side of the head with everything I had, which was enough, because he went down into what used to be my pizza.

That left the other two guys, and feeling brave and cocksure from my below-the-belt victory over the one in the quilted jacket, I went after the stocky guy in the cowhide, who had been standing near the mouth of the alley opposite the guy clutching Kathy, watching in case anybody tried to get involved (in Chicago?). I dove at him and he swatted me like a fly, over into some garbage cans.

I hit hard, only it sounded worse than it felt, and I saw Kathy's eyes get even wider and more frightened, and the stocky guy came after me with a nasty smile and two outstretched arms that weren't planning to hug me, at least not in any affectionate way. I reached for something and my hand found the handle of a garbage can lid. I smacked him in the chest with it, like Prince Valiant using his shield on a barbarian. He went back on his ass, but sprang right up—and into my second roundhouse swing of the garbage can lid, which his face put a nice dent in.

He went down and out.

I turned and looked at the kid holding Kathy; I was splattered with blood and garbage and former pizza, and I had the dented garbage can lid in my hand and must've looked meaner than I thought, because he let go of her and ran.

"Let's get the cops!" Kathy said.

I reached down and pulled the wallet out of the stocky guy's pocket and checked his ID; he had a couple of business cards, and I took one of them.

Kathy was holding onto my arm now, and I grinned at her. "Was it me that said Gat Garson wasn't a good role model?"

She had hysteria in her eyes. "Didn't you hear me? Let's get the damn cops!"

"What, and lose you your job?" I said.

"What do you mean?"

148

I pointed at the two unconscious men.

"Haven't you ever seen angels before?"

She didn't know what I was talking about, but the confusion helped; we were in the first passing cab before she knew it.

14

WE never did make it to Old Town that Friday night; we didn't get to use those coveted reservations at Second City. I was bloody and just generally a mess, and Kathy was more or less hysterical herself, so we took the cab back to the hotel and ended up in my room. I was sorry we were going to miss North Wells Street and the funky shops and the good restaurants and the great show at Second City; but not sorry that I was alone in my room with Kathy Wickman.

Who even now was sitting on my bed.

"I knew Gregg was a sleazy little son of a bitch," she said, gesticulating, "but I never *dreamed* him capable of *this*."

"Of what?" I said. I was standing in the bathroom at the sink, trying to decide whether to apply a cold washcloth to where my lip had gotten cut when I'd crashed into the garbage cans.

"Of sending people to beat you up," she said, a little irritated with my offhand attitude. Back in the cab I'd shown her the business card I'd lifted off one of the two guys in the alley, a card identifying him as Harry DiAngeli, DiAngeli Adult Books, Inc. Which made him an angel a couple of ways, neither of which would carry much weight with St. Peter, I felt sure.

150

I came out and took my shirt off, and I was not, I assure you, doing my Richard Gere impression. While I have a certain amount of hair on my chest, no woman's ever fainted over it, and I never owned a gold chain in my life. I was just anxious to change out of what might be described as a Gino's pizza T-shirt.

"I thought," I said, slipping a gray short-sleeve sweatshirt on, "you might have been referring to that other little thing Gorman seems to be up to."

Her mouth twitched thoughtfully. "You mean that Hammett book."

I sat on the edge of the bed next to her. "I mean that most probably fraudulent Hammett book."

She touched my cut lip, with absentminded compassion. "And you think that has something to do with Roscoe Kane's death?"

"Let me put it this way: Gorman went to the trouble of having his angels publicly assault us. Not that anyone in Chicago seemed to take notice, but still."

"Your point being?"

"Look. I'm not saying Gorman isn't capable of doing that just out of spite. That fallen angel of his *did* make sure I took a good shot in the gut, you know, to even the score."

She thought that over. "But he also told you to get out of town."

"*That's* my point. He did everything but put me on a stagecoach."

"But, why?"

"Elementary, my dear Wickman. I'm looking into Roscoe Kane's untimely demise. The local authorities have written Kane off as an accidental death. My poking around might be enough to get the matter reopened, if I'm stubborn and noisy enough about it.

And Gorman knows me to be both plenty stubborn and just a little bit noisy."

She was very, very pale; and, while it was barely perceptible, shaking some. "And you think Gregg is capable of . . .?"

"Murder? Who knows what evil lurks?"

"How can you be so flip about it?"

"About murder? Death? Ah, shucks, ma'am. Trouble is my business. I go around on the prowl for homicide, just so I can put it all down on paper and make a bundle. I'm looking for another movie-of-the-week out of this one."

She studied me.

"This flipness," she said. "You're masking how you *really* feel, aren't you? Roscoe Kane's death is a real blow to you, isn't it. . . ."

I got up. I went over and pushed on my cassette player. Bobby Darin started singing "Beyond the Sea." I loved that song, but these days it made me melancholy. Ever since Darin died, that song always got me to thinking in metaphorical terms. *Somewhere—beyond the sea* . . . I looked out the window down at Michigan Avenue and the adjacent park; I could see it all very well, but the street lights made it seem unreal, artificial. Street sounds floated up, seeming muffled and clear at the same time. Underwater sounds.

Without looking back at her, I said, "The hell of it is, if I do figure out what happened to Roscoe, and who did it . . . and *why* . . . he'll still be dead. And someday so will I, and someday so will you. So what's the point? What's the goddamn fucking point?"

I felt her hand on my arm; cool.

I hadn't even heard her get out of bed, let alone cross the room to me. I looked back at her. She didn't have the pink Norma Kamali top on anymore.

"Who says there has to be any point?" she asked.

I looked at her breasts. Or, as Gat might say, her perfect B cups were like two generous scoops of vanilla ice cream, each topped with a cherry.

"If there's no point," I said, with an involuntary smile, "then don't point those things at me."

"'Cause they might be loaded, Gat?" she asked, smiling wryly (#569) and then tumbled into my arms.

She looked at me with a face so pretty it made my teeth hurt. She said, "Why don't you forget this stupid mess and just enjoy the 'con and my company and then go home? You can spend the better part of the next two days in bed with me."

"I've had worse offers."

"Have you had better?"

Not ever. She was sweeter than Gat Garson's silly ice-cream metaphor. She was a tonic for all that ailed me. She was a hundred pounds or so of affection with shimmering brown hair and shimmering brown eyes and holding her in my arms made me not give a goddamn whether there was any point to life or death, or infinity either, for that matter.

"Isn't this when they smoke in books?" she asked. She was sitting up in bed, with both pillows behind her, sheet and blankets around her waist. The ice-cream scoops were tilting up; it'd be years before they started to melt.

"It sure is. Only I don't smoke."

"Neither do I."

"Then let's not."

"Okay."

"Besides," I said, "we don't want to indulge in too many clichés. We've just had the obligatory sex scene. And we've already had the ritual violence."

Curiosity tinged her wry smile. "What d'you mean, 'ritual violence'?"

153

"Gorman's business associates running that tough-guy number. It was right on cue. You have to have a little action, in a private eye yarn."

"Is that what this is?"

Outside the window, a siren—ambulance, prob-ably—split the night open.

"That seems to be what I'm trying to make it," I said. "If I were writing this, I'd be tempted to leave out the sex scene, and the ritual violence, too. They might play okay, but they've been done to death. So I'd probably cut 'em. Kill your darlings, y'know."

"What?"

I grinned at her. "You never heard that old bromide? The editor of *Noir?* Shame on ya. That's the mystery writers' code."

"Kill your darlings?"

"Sure. It's just a way of saying to a writer: cut your work, ruthlessly; edit it, unsparingly. Get rid of the self-indulgent crap. I first heard that vivid little piece of advice from Roscoe Kane when he was showing me where to cut my first novel."

She cocked her head, a good-natured, puzzled expression on her face. "I'm still not sure I get it. . . ."

I leaned on one elbow, gestured with my other hand, pretending to be smart. "Y'see, often the things writers get the biggest charge out of in their own stories—a mixed metaphor here, a purple phrase there, even a complete scene full of snappy but pointless patter—are exactly what ought to be slashed the hell outta there. Of course, if I cut all the self-indulgences out of *my* novels, they'd be short stories. Still, like the old mystery writer says, kill your darlings—only the Roscoe Kane Murder Case is so full of self-indulgences on my part, I'm starting to think the whole damn thing might be invalid."

"Don't be silly, Mal. . . ."

I stole one of the pillows out from behind her so I could sit up in bed comfortably, too. Postcoital chivalry may not be dead, but it clearly isn't feeling well.

I said, "It's like Sardini, and even Gorman, said: I've read too many mysteries. And maybe written too many, too."

She studied me.

I said, "I'd appreciate it if you'd violently disagree with that last point."

Little smile. "Consider yourself violently disagreed with."

"Thanks. Coming from the heart as that did, it means a lot. Anyway, maybe I *should* throw in the towel on this one."

"Like Roscoe Kane's killer did."

"Huh?"

She poked at my chest with a tapered finger. "He threw the towel in, remember? Actually, plural, towels. In the hamper. Sopped up the water with 'em after drowning Kane . . . remember? Your theory?"

I got out of bed and walked over to the window again; Darin was singing "Artificial Flowers," a satirically upbeat song about a little girl who freezes to death selling flowers on a street corner.

"That's just what I mean, Kathy," I said, looking down at the unreal street. "That's so damn lame. That's mystery-novel evidence, not real-life evidence. No, I should try to accept the possibility . . . the likelihood . . . that Roscoe really did die an accidental death. I'm deluding myself into thinking he was murdered, because in a way, it's keeping him alive for me."

This time I heard her crossing the room behind me, as she said, "How so, Mal?"

I turned and looked at her; the only light in the room came from the window behind us and the

155

shadows and dim lighting gave her lithe little body that same glow of unreality as the street below.

"Don't you get it?" I asked her. "As long as I'm playing Gat Garson, trying to sort out Roscoe's death, then Roscoe's still with us, in a way ... till his 'murder' is solved, his life remains unresolved. His story unfinished. Which may be how I want it."

She stroked my arm. "That's not true. You're *trying* to solve that murder, resolve that life. You're not trying to hold onto Roscoe Kane in some sick, sub-conscious way. You're just following that sweet, silly romantic nature of yours—trying to make sense out of things, make life—and death—*mean* something. That may be a hopeless pursuit, but it's a ... noble one."

"You talk like a character in a G. Roger Donaldson book," I said, with a small smile.

The one-sided smile she gave me back looked sad in the half-light. "Maybe I've read too many mystery novels, too."

I hugged her. "You're the only real thing that's happened to me at this place. Everything else is like a bad dream."

She nibbled at my ear. "You said I was a dream come true, in bed."

"Wet dream come true, I meant to say."

"Gat, you say such sweetly tacky things. . . ."

We stood and looked at each other; smiled at each other. Walked hand in hand back to the bed and crawled under the covers. Cuddled like spoons.

"I don't know, Kathy," I said to her back. "I think maybe I've just been running a scam on myself, a bigger scam even than Gorman's."

She glanced over her shoulder at me. "But *that* you believe is real. Gorman's scam."

"Sure. And I believe Roscoe probably ghosted that book for him; I'll know for sure when I read it."

She studied me.

I went on. "If Roscoe *did* ghost it, Gorman obviously wouldn't want me, or anybody, poking around where Roscoe Kane is concerned, 'cause the scam might come out in the open—where, as Gat Garson would say, it'd unravel like a cheap sweater."

"Wouldn't it eventually come out anyway?"

"Timing here is everything. If the book goes to publication, and a controversy follows, so do major sales for the book. Years ago that happened with something called *The Search for Bridey Murphy*, which you're too young to remember. But if the controversy precedes publication—if in fact, the hoax is exposed *before* publication—the book's dead in the water. Pardon the expression. And so's Gorman."

"Wouldn't people still want to read the thing?"

"Some people would; but not many. And it probably wouldn't even go to press—the publisher would be too embarrassed about the incident. Remember the Clifford Irving/Howard Hughes 'autobiography'?"

She turned over and faced me. "I see what you mean. And Gregg might've gotten concerned about his ghost, Kane, getting talkative . . . Kane *was* drinking heavily again, after all, and in public—and you did say Kane was talking wild in the bar, last night. . . ."

I nodded. "And Gorman could've thought Roscoe's loose lips might sink the Hammett ship—yeah. That's a real possibility. . . ."

"You're not going to stop looking into this, are you, Mal?"

Bobby Darin was singing "Mack the Knife" in the background: *Oh, the shark, babe . . .*

"No," I said. "I don't have it in me to let this lie. I wish I did."

"I'm glad you don't."

"I'm afraid, Kathy."

"What of? Gorman and his goons?"

"Watch it," I cautioned her. "Now you're starting to sound like some dame in a Gat Garson novel."

I motioned over at the cover painting against the wall; I'd turned it face out when we came in, earlier. In the half-light the girl on the *Murder Me Again, Doll* cover looked frighteningly like Kathy.

"After that scene in the alley," she said, "I *feel* like a character in a Gat Garson novel."

I put a hand on an ice-cream scoop. "You do at that."

She smiled one-sidedly and said, "And I suppose you have Gat Garson's recuperative powers?"

"Sexually speaking you mean?"

"Sexually speaking is exactly what I mean."

"When Gat was asked something very similar, in *Death Is a Dame,* he said, 'Baby, you could raise the dead.'"

"Why don't you show me what happens next in a Kane novel, after such racy double-entendres ensue?"

"I can't."

"Oh?"

"No, doll. See, at this point Kane always fades out. . . ."

Pretty soon I was being wakened by a light going on in the bathroom. I opened my eyes—or anyway, one eye—and saw Kathy in there, fully dressed, freshening up at the sink.

"Are you going somewhere?" I asked.

I gave her a start; wide-eyed, she said, "I, uh . . . need to go to Gorman's party. Nightcaps after the movie, remember?"

I sat up in bed. "Why are you doing that, for Christ's sake?"

She stood in the bathroom doorway, a silhouette against the light behind her. "He's still my publisher, after all."

I thought about that.

Then said, "What are you up to?"

"I have to make an appearance," she said. "*Noir*'s important to me. . . ."

She was passing by the bed, and I latched onto her wrist. Not hard. But hard enough to stop her.

"You're not that crass," I said. "You're pissed about what those angels of his did to us, and you're up to something. *What?*"

She pulled her arm away from my grip.

"Go to sleep," she said.

"What are you up to?"

"Can I have a key so I can come back and join you, later? Or would you rather I slept in my own room?"

"Don't leave, Kathy. Just stay put."

Very firmly she said, "Can I have a key, Mal?"

"There's one on the dresser. Take it. Want me to go with you?"

"So you can punch Gregg in the stomach again? No thanks. Trust me on this, Mal."

"Do I have a choice?"

"No," she said, shaking her head no.

"Well," I said. "Have fun."

Wry smile #892. "See what I can do. Mal?"

"Yeah?"

"Before we got . . . sidetracked, you said . . . said you were afraid. What of?"

"Oh. Nothing."

"Come on. Spill."

I shrugged. "Finding Roscoe's killer, if there is such a person. It's not going to make anything right, you

159

know. That's when it's really going to hit me. That Roscoe's dead and all my fancy footwork didn't really do him any good."

"Don't say that."

"Why not?"

" 'Cause it isn't true. Do you *really* think Gat Garson would want this mystery left unsolved?"

I smiled uneasily. "I guess not. Or Roscoe either."

"Right. I'll see you a little later."

And she was gone.

I tried to go back to sleep, without much luck. I checked the TV, and there was an old Bowery Boys movie on—*Dig That Uranium*—and I watched it and, God bless Huntz Hall and Leo Gorcey, I forgot my problems (except during the interminable commercials, during one spate of which I slipped some trousers on and went out and got a couple of cans of 7-Up from the machine down the hall).

I was still watching when the door opened and Kathy came back in. She had something under her arm.

"What you got there?" I asked, sitting in my shorts, Leo Gorcey beating Huntz Hall over the head with his hat, on the glowing tube behind me.

"You said you thought you'd read too many mystery novels," she said, tossing something at me. "Think you got it in you to read one more?"

It was a manuscript, in a brown folder. A photocopy of a manuscript, that is; running over two hundred pages.

"Be done with that by morning, will you?" she said, getting ready for bed by climbing out of her clothes and crawling in.

On the title page of the manuscript, it said, "*The Secret Emperor* by Dashiell Hammett."

She snored.

I read.

Part Three:
SATURDAY

15

THE Bouchercon folks had switched me from one panel ("The State of the Mystery") at nine o'clock to another panel ("Whither the Private Eye") at eleven. So, because I'd been up most of the night reading, I slept in till ten. Kathy was up and gone when I awoke; so was the Hammett manuscript. But she'd left a note saying she'd gone back to her room to make herself presentable for the day.

I called her.

"I'd just about given up on you," she said.

"I was up all night with a good book."

"So it *is* good?"

"Very. But that's all I'd care to say about it for the moment."

"Be that way. I, uh, returned it to Gregg."

"How did he happen to have a copy of it along, anyway?"

"He didn't, exactly. It was a copy that G. Roger Donaldson returned to Gregg."

"Oh, yeah? Why did Donaldson have a copy?"

"He and Gregg are thick, I understand. I never met Donaldson—he was supposed to be at the party last night, but he didn't show. Anyway, Donaldson is one of the 'experts' who verified the work as legitimate

Hammett for Gregg. Gregg had some heavy people in the field put their opinions in writing, so he could attach copies when he sent the manuscript around to the various major publishers last month, for auction."

"What's Donaldson's connection to Gorman?"

"Gregg's publishing a book by Donaldson."

That didn't sound right. "What's a big name like Donaldson doing with a small publisher like Mystery House?"

"It's a collection of short stories; Donaldson's regular publisher declined it—you know how that goes, short-story collections being notoriously poor sellers."

"So you sneaked the manuscript out of Gorman's room last night, huh? Nice work."

"Nothing so subversive as that. Gregg gave it to me so I could do an advance write-up for *Noir*. I told him last night I was hyper-anxious to see *The Secret Emperor* and asked him to let me read it overnight."

"I appreciate this, Kathy."

"Then buy me breakfast. Meet you outside the coffee shop?"

I beat her down there. Sardini, looking pale and bleary-eyed, approached me; his shirt was tucked in, which was quite an accomplishment for a guy who'd obviously had even less sleep than I had.

"Where'd you disappear to last night?" he asked.

"Us country folk know how to have us a good time in the big city."

"You couldn't've had a good time last night without us knowing about it. Ed and I must've hit every bar in the Loop."

Ed Charterman, eyes behind his wire-frame glasses looking almost as bleary as Tom's, wandered up to us; he was a New York editor who'd been at several publishing houses, and was one of the better editors in the business—an opinion I held despite his never having bought anything of mine.

He dug some cigarettes out from the pocket of his plaid shirt, smirked and nodded at us (which meant hello) and had a cigarette for breakfast.

"You gonna join us?" Charterman asked me, motioning toward the Gazebo.

"I would," I said, "but I only eat with editors who buy my stories."

He shrugged, gave me a pleasantly cynical smile. "You must pay for most of your own meals."

Kathy exited the elevators and waved at me and headed our way; under his breath, Sardini said, "You country boys do know how to have a good time in the big city."

"Easy," I said. "That's the woman I love you're talking about." Funny thing was, I think I meant it.

Kathy was wearing another *Noir* shirt, a red polo shirt with the deco lettering in white, and white jeans.

I introduced everybody (both Tom and Ed knew Kathy by name and rep but never met her before) and we went in for breakfast, taking one of the covered booths at the far side of the place.

Breakfast conversation was pleasant, but superficial; Tom didn't mention Roscoe Kane's death, but he did tell me that my two run-ins with Gorman were the talk of the convention. Kathy shot me a furtive look, wondering if I'd tell about our angelic visitation last night outside of Gino's. I didn't.

"Do me a favor," Tom said, "and check with Mae Kane for me. She isn't answering her phone, and I don't want to go knocking on her door at a time like this. But I need to make sure she's at the PWA awards this afternoon, to accept that Life Achievement Award for her husband."

"She'll be there," I said.

"And I'd like you to present the award. Sorry for the short notice—"

"I'd be upset if I *didn't* get to present this award. I won't pretend otherwise."

Across the coffee shop, a short, broad-shouldered man in a lime-colored blazer and black slacks, a dark green handkerchief in the blazer pocket, sauntered toward us. He had thinning reddish blond hair, and a round face and a full beard; he looked like a cross between Ernest Hemingway and one of the Beach Boys.

I'd never met this man but I recognized him, from his bookjackets and TV appearances.

"G. Roger Donaldson," I said.

He came up to us and smiled tightly, meaninglessly, at Tom, Ed and me, then focused on Kathy.

"You'd be Ms. Wickman," he said. He had a clipped voice, like every word was the last squeeze out of a toothpaste tube.

"That's right," Kathy said, smiling, impressed. "And you'd be G. Roger Donaldson."

He nodded; no "Call me Roger." Not even call me "G."

But Kathy was awestruck; she tried to stand up in the booth, which wasn't easy, but she was short enough to sort of accomplish it. Reaching across our breakfasts, they shook hands.

In his measured way, Donaldson delivered the following speech: "I just wanted to say how perceptive I thought your comments were on my current novel. It amazes me how my simple imaginative constructs can so mystify some critics. Your critique, on the other hand, was right on target."

And with a courtly little bow, he moved off to a side table, and sat and waved a waiter over for coffee.

Kathy was beaming. "What a nice thing to say. Elegant man."

"Yeah," I said. "Real elegant of him to agree with your rave of his new book." Despite many accolades for all of his books, Donaldson was beginning to slip in the estimation of some critics.

"You're just jealous," she said.

"Yeah," Tom said, "you wish you had a sports coat like that."

"Actually," Charterman said, "he wishes he could *afford* a sports coat like that."

I couldn't disagree.

Kathy wasn't through. "Why do you dislike Donaldson so much, Mal?"

"I don't dislike him. I never met him—including just now, if you were paying attention. But I do dislike what he represents—pompous posturing in a field best known for straightforward storytelling."

"I liked his first books—" Tom shrugged. He was concentrating more on his plate of pancakes than this conversation.

"In fairness," I said, "I have to admit I never finished a Donaldson novel. The tortured similies and the neo-macho attitudes were too much for me. I have no time for a mystery writer who wants to be Norman Mailer when he grows up. As a matter of fact, I have no time for Norman Mailer, who after all wants to be Ernest Hemingway when he grows up. And I even get impatient with Hemingway, 'cause he obviously wanted to be Joseph Conrad when *he* grew up. . . ."

Charterman, cutting some bacon, said, "Stop him before he gets to Chaucer, or this'll turn into Darwin's theory of evolution."

Kathy folded her arms and gave me a look of mock irritation. "Could we go now? I don't think I want to

167

be seen with a writer who wants to be Roscoe Kane when he grows up."

Tom said, "Who wants to grow up?" and kept eating his pancakes.

We went to the Gold Room; the panel was due to start in fifteen minutes. In the front row of the massive high-ceilinged ornate room, Kathy found a seat just a few feet from the stage, across which stretched a long table decorated with microphones and glasses of water.

Peter Christian was the moderator of the panel, and I spotted him in the wings, stage left. Knowing Pete, he'd probably been up later than both Sardini and Charterman, but he looked less bleary-eyed than either. Pete always looked like he'd just crawled out from under a collapsed building, without seeming any the worse for wear. He smiled as I approached him.

"I've been looking forward to this panel," he said, holding a hand out for me to shake, even though I'd seen him the day before. "I feel quite delighted to've been asked to moderate, since I'm not from Chicago. One of their own, by all rights, should do the honors."

"They just know a class act when they see one," I said, meaning it.

Pete laughed a little, as though my remark had been sarcastic. He said, "My only worry is Donaldson."

"Oh?"

Pete ran a hand over his head; he always managed to look tired and alert at the same time, seem simultaneously harried and calm, laid-back and energetic.

He said, "I'm told the guy *thought* he'd have the panel to himself . . . a one-man show."

"Well," I said, shrugging, "he *is* the guest of honor, after all. He probably should've had it to himself."

"No," Pete said, shaking his head. "Too many writers here who deserve to be on panels. The fans like to see a lot of faces."

"Even this face?"

"Sure, why not? I think you, Sardini and Donaldson make an interesting grouping."

"I thought Bill Pronzini was going to be on our panel."

"Didn't you hear? That's who you're filling in for. Bill dislikes Donaldson's work so much that when he heard the man was going to be guest of honor, he stayed home in San Francisco, by way of protest."

"No kidding?"

"No kidding."

Pretty soon Pete and Tom and I were sitting behind the table on the platform; the room was packed. Everybody at the Bouchercon was here—except the guest of honor.

After five minutes, the crowd getting restless and noisy, Pete began: "I guess we'll have to go ahead and get started. G. Roger Donaldson is supposed to be with us, as you all know, but—"

Then down the center aisle Donaldson rolled, like a little Patton. He nodded smilingly at either side of him as he moved along, acknowledging his troops.

He joined us at the table.

"Well"—Pete smiled—"speak of the devil. . . ."

The crowd laughed, and Donaldson stood, and nodded at the crowd, who began to applaud him. Sardini and I exchanged looks; now we knew what it was like to be Moe and Larry—Donaldson was clearly the most popular stooge present.

Pete asked various questions, which each of us got to answer, all on the basic subject "Whither the Private Eye," which was to say, what was the current state, and probably future, of the modern private eye novel.

Sardini talked about being a fan of private eye fiction, and dreaming of being a published writer of private eye fiction himself one day, and working hard at, and finally achieving, that goal.

I talked about having been an aspiring mystery writer who became involved in several real-life crimes, and how my method in my first two books had been to bring some of the techniques of the private eye/mystery novel to a fact-based work.

Donaldson talked about using the private eye novel as a vehicle for his art ("If I may be so bold as to exhalt my work as such") so that he might explore love relationships, male bonding, ethical and moral issues, etc.

It went on like that: Tom and I would talk about plot, Donaldson would talk about epiphany; Tom and I would talk about character, Donaldson would talk about objective correlatives. Did I mention Donaldson teaches literature? At Berkeley?

Finally it was opened up to the audience.

"Mr. Donaldson," an earnest young woman in a deerstalker cap said, "what is your opinion of Hammett and Chandler?"

A hush fell across the room; the great was about to pronounce judgment on the great.

Donaldson leaned forward; pursing his lips, he gave his measured assessment as follows: "Hammett wrote one very good book, one competent book, and three very bad books. Oh, and I happen to have had an advance look at the newly discovered novel, and it's one of his better works. Of course, Chandler was by far the superior author, although a limited one. He wrote the same book seven times, after all. I think the modern artist using the private eye story as a vehicle for his art has to thank both these men—but must attempt to go far beyond them."

Some of the faces out there wore looks of annoyance, a few people seemed amused, but most heads were nodding.

I spoke up. I wasn't asked, but when did that ever stop me?

I said, "It's magnanimous of G. Roger, here, to thank Hammett and Chandler. It's quite a startling declaration. If Hammett and Chandler were here today, they might say, 'Gee, Roger—you're welcome.'"

Donaldson turned and looked at me, past an amused-but-trying-to-hide-it Pete Christian; it was the first time Donaldson had looked my way, and the first time he'd recognized that I was his enemy. He had money-green eyes that were on me like death rays.

He said, coldly, "I meant no disrespect to Hammett and Chandler . . . only that in the literary overview, their work needs to be placed in perspective."

I said, coolly, "Where, in the literary overview, would you place yourself?"

With a one-sided smile and a wag of his round head, he feigned self-deprecation. "That's not for me to say. I would hope posterity would notice me—but I'm not counting on it."

Tom said, "Posterity pays lousy royalties."

That got a laugh from the crowd, and Donaldson pretended to be amused, too.

Another question from the crowd, this from Brett Murtz: "What is your opinion of Roscoe Kane's Gat Garson stories?"

Another hush fell over the room.

Donaldson smiled that meaningless smile again and shook his round head. "It is perhaps in bad taste for me to respond. But . . . the Gat Garson books are beneath contempt, really. Badly done—the main character, cardboard; not rounded. Nobody cares about Gat Garson. I rank Kane just above Spillane—which is faint praise indeed."

Murtz, still standing, said, "Well, how would you characterize your own character, Keats, then?"

Donaldson smiled broadly and with no self-deprecation at all said, "Rounded, fully dimensional, caring, committed, beguiling—and good-looking."

Most everyone out there was smiling at this horse-flop.

Donaldson went on: "The private eye story, remember, is useful to me only as a way to explore certain aspects of human life. I am attempting in my work to go where no private eye writer has gone before. . . ."

"You do realize you're quoting *Star Trek*," I said, interrupting, "don't you?"

A hush *really* fell over the room, though there were some smiles and stifled laughter.

Donaldson wasn't smiling, however, or laughing. Just staring—unlike his fictional private eye, he did not have a fast comeback for me. So I said my piece.

"Mr. Donaldson," I said, "I sat by and listened to you dismiss three of Dashiell Hammett's books as 'very bad.' I listened as you tossed off Chandler as somebody who wrote the same book seven times. And I sat quietly as you verbally looked down your literary nose at Mickey Spillane, at the same time having the indecency to condemn Roscoe Kane before his body's had a chance to cool. But I don't care to listen to G.

172

Roger Donaldson on the subject of G. Roger Donaldson, thank you."

Donaldson, his face white where it wasn't bearded, looked at me with those green death-ray eyes full of contempt.

"Excuse me," I said to the crowd.

And I walked off the stage.

Kathy, running, caught up with me at the mouth of the down escalator.

"You were right about that jerk," she said.

"I've sure been keeping my cool at this 'con," I said, feeling ashamed and silly. I got on the escalator. She got on behind me.

"Tom Sardini's right," she admitted, putting her head on my shoulder, talking into my ear. "You *are* the talk of the convention."

"As in, 'What an embarrassing ass that guy Mallory is'?"

She shrugged. "Some of it runs like that."

"Well, you ain't seen nothin' yet," I said.

"What do you mean?"

"Wait till this afternoon."

"Oh?"

"Yeah," I said. "When I publicly announce Roscoe Kane ghosted the Hammett book."

16

I KNOCKED ON Mae Kane's door. Kathy was with me, feeling a little awkward, she said, about meeting Roscoe Kane's recent widow. We were about to go out for some lunch, but I dragged her along with me to room 714, first. I needed to check in with Mae, as I'd promised Tom Sardini I would; had to make sure she'd be at the PWA awards ceremony at two o'clock.

Of course she didn't answer right away; the do-not-disturb sign still hung on the knob, and she'd told me herself she'd gotten gun-shy from media people and well-meaning fans bugging her—and Tom had said she wasn't answering her phone for anybody.

But I knew she was in there, so I kept at it.

"Mae, it's Mal," I said as I knocked.

And finally she cracked the door open; the Joan Crawford eyes were perfectly mascaraed and the red filigree largely gone. She smiled at me over the nightlatch chain, and she said, huskily, "Mal . . . I'd hoped you'd come by. But it's a bad time. . . ."

Then she noticed Kathy and her expression turned cool. "I don't believe we've met," she said. To neither one of us in particular; just to the air.

"This is Kathy Wickman," I said. "A good friend of mine. Kathy, this is Mae Kane."

Kathy stepped forward and held out her hand, but with the door still only cracked open, nightlatch chain still in place, the well-intentioned gesture fell flat.

Kathy withdrew the hand, smiled sympathetically and said, "I'm very sorry about your husband. He'll be missed."

"Well, I'll miss him," Mae said, defensively, as if Kathy had implied she wouldn't.

"Mae," I said, wondering if she'd been hitting the gin, "are you all right?"

She found a warm smile for me. "Fine. Just kind of . . . tied up. Can you stop by later?" Kathy was obviously excluded from the latter invitation.

"Sure," I said, and then Mae looked startled, and suddenly her face disappeared from the cracked door, which closed, abruptly, and the sound of the night-latch being unchained hastily was followed by the door opening wide.

And Gregg Gorman was standing there.

Wearing, ironically enough, a black *Noir* T-shirt.

He pointed a finger at Kathy, thrust a finger at Kathy.

"What are you doing with *him?*" he demanded.

He meant me, of course; he sounded like a Ku Klux Klan kleagle who found his daughter Ellie Lou listening to Johnny Mathis records.

Kathy raised her eyebrows in that equivalent of a shrug and said, "Just along for the ride. We were on our way to lunch."

"Care to join us, Gregg?" I asked. "We'll find a place with a trough."

Some 'con attendees (badges pinned to chests) came wandering down the hall, talking about how terrific G. Roger Donaldson was. Mindful of a scene, Gorman made a hurried gesture toward Mae's room. Mae was in there somewhere, presumably; she had disappeared from view.

We didn't heed his gesture.

He tried again. "Step in," he said. Forcing a civil tone into his thin, unpleasant voice. "I want to talk to you two."

I looked at Kathy and she made a shrugging face at me again and I made one back, and we walked into Mae's room.

Mae was standing in the bathroom, her face ashen; standing next to the tub where Roscoe drowned.

"Well, Gorman," I said, "visiting the scene of the crime, I see. Morbid curiosity, or a return trip?"

He held two vaguely dirty palms up, like a referee. "I had nothing to do with that. I swear."

"What are you doing here, Gorman? What's he *doing* here, Mae?"

She stepped out of the bathroom; the arcs of silver hair swung with the rhythm of her body. Her supple body, as Gat Garson would say. Which today was sheathed in black, a clingy, attractive black; widow's weeds weren't what they used to be.

"Mal," she said. "I know how you feel about Gregg. I wanted to avoid a confrontation . . ."

"What's he doing here, Mae? What are you doing here, Gorman?"

Gorman shrugged; he was like a kid caught cheating on a test in school. "Business."

Mae chimed in brightly. "It's about Roscoe's books. He wants to do a boxed set of Roscoe's first six Gat Garsons. I suggested you for the introductions—"

"But," Gorman said, picking up the ball, "I told her you'd probably turn me down. 'Cause you hate my guts."

"I don't hate your guts. I'm not that selective."

Gorman's face turned beet red, everywhere that wasn't covered by his unsanitary goatee; oddly, his drinker's nose seemed a lighter shade of red than the rest of his face.

But the anger I'd generated—or thought I'd generated—didn't get vented on me.

Instead, he whirled toward Kathy and pointed a finger gunlike at her and said, "You little bitch, what's the idea of—"

I took him by the small of the arm and walked him a couple of steps like a friend I was counseling; he looked at me with big eyes and open mouth, wondering what the hell.

"I'm having a bad weekend, Gregg," I said, calmly. "I think I'm having a nervous breakdown or something. I'm punching people in the stomach, hitting people with garbage can lids, walking off panels in a huff—in a minute and a huff, as Groucho would say. I'm feeling so out-of-sorts, I'm liable to start breaking you up into kindling if you continue going 'round calling people 'bitch' and 'asshole' and the like."

And I smiled and let him go, and he pulled away from me, gave me an indignant look. "You *are* cracking up. Do you know who you're fooling with? Do you know?"

"I know," I said. "I was in the alley last night, with your angels who deal in dirty pictures. They're mob-dirty, too, but I don't think anybody's going to kill me just because I'm not nice to you, Gregg."

"Don't be too sure," he said. "Don't be too sure."

Mae's Joan Crawford eyes went ultra-wide. "Gregg! What are you *saying*! I won't have you talking to Mal that way—he's my friend, and he was my husband's protégé, and—"

"Sorry, Mae," Gorman said, the anger still pulsing in his red face. "Just lost my temper a second."

Kathy, who'd been uncharacteristically quiet, probably because she was scared out of her skin, found the presence to say, in clipped tones, "You wanted to ask me something, Mr. Gorman. What is it?"

Gorman smiled, pretending to swallow his anger; but there was too much of it to take in in one gulp. He was wholly unconvincing when he went to her and patted her shoulder, paternally, saying, "Mr. Gorman. What nonsense is that? We're friends, we been friends for years. I'm sorry I snapped at you, baby."

"Don't call me 'baby,'" Kathy said. Through her teeth.

"Kathy. Look, darlin'. I just want to ask you something. You lied to me, didn't ya? You said you and Mallory weren't seeing each other."

"Is that the question?"

"No, hon. It's . . . something else. You, uh, didn't . . . last night, when you borrowed that . . . you didn't give it to . . ."

I smiled cheerfully and said, "I think *The Secret Emperor* is a hell of a book. Really I do. It's just too bad Dashiell Hammett didn't write it."

"Shit!" Gorman said, his rage-red mask returning, frustration mixed in with the anger. "Shit." He turned and walked away from us, pacing in the area between the bed and the wall.

Mae came up to me and said, "I don't understand, Mal. Are you talking about the newly discovered—"

"Save it, Mae. I think I know the business you and Gregg were discussing."

"Wh-what do you mean?"

"Roscoe Kane wrote the Hammett book. I read it last night. It's wonderful. It's perhaps Roscoe's masterpiece—the only thing that makes me say 'perhaps' is that it's not a Gat Garson book, but a Continental

Op story. A pastiche. Which makes it automatically a lesser work, but . . ."

Gorman turned and with two raised fists shaking in the air said, "Go to hell!" Then he lowered the fists and looked at the floor and said, "Go to hell."

I moved away from Mae and toward Gorman; Kathy stood quietly, nervously by the door.

I said, "I meant no sarcasm by what I said, Gorman. I really do think the book is a remarkable work. Where mystery writers are concerned, Hammett was the best. And Roscoe Kane was second-best. I've always felt that way; I always ranked him above Chandler and the rest—though most people have told me I'm nuts for having that opinion. But you and I have something in common, Gorman. A common bond, yessir."

He sat, on the edge of Mae's bed; he looked up at me with empty eyes. The hate had drained out; he seemed tired, slumped there on the edge of the bed. Even his goatee looked limp.

I said, "You and I, we both knew. We both knew just how good Roscoe was. We both knew how thoroughly he admired Hammett, how much he'd studied him. And we both know he may have been the only writer alive who could convincingly, seamlessly, pick up the ball for ol' Dash."

And Gorman started to smile. Just a little.

"I don't know what you're talking about," he said, lightly.

"Oh? That's your stand, is it? Just going to tough it out. You figure I can't prove it; it's an allegation I can make, but can't prove, and since Roscoe Kane's so underestimated a writer, even so maligned a writer, my allegation will seem foolish. 'Roscoe Kane pass for Dashiell Hammett? Don't be absurd!' That what you expect?"

"You'll look the fool you are, Mallory." He didn't look as tired now.

"I think you're wrong," I said. "I think I can prove Kane wrote *The Secret Emperor*. I can certainly raise enough doubt to cause you a lot of trouble. You see, you know Kane's work well, but not as well as I do. He gave me something, once. An unpublished early novel of his. He said it was a darling he should've killed. Never mind what he meant by that. Suffice to say it was a book no publisher had wanted but that he'd always had a fondness for. And rather than throw it out, he gave it to me, his fan, his 'protégé,' if you will."

Gorman, not following this, smiled uneasily and said, "So?"

"So, it isn't a terrific book—but it's a nice book. And four of the major characters and one subplot from that unpublished novel found their way into his Hammett pastiche, the novel you're passing off as *The Secret Emperor*."

Gorman's face went white; he exchanged quick glances with an equally white Mae Kane.

"He did that on purpose," I said. "At least that's my instinct. He wanted to leave a clue for somebody—specifically me—so that one day his authorship would be established. You see, I think he agreed to go along with your hoax—complete the five-thousand word manuscript of Hammett's that's sitting down in the University of Texas collection, even as we speak—for his own purposes."

Mae said, "Mal, if Roscoe ghosted that book, it's news to me. . . ."

I turned and looked at her. "That's what you wanted me to think; that's why you told me about Roscoe being troubled about something in recent months, something he hadn't shared with you. If I stumbled onto the truth, you didn't want to seem to be a part of it. Did you, Mae?"

"Mal, you're wrong—so wrong. . . ."

"No, Mae, I'm right. This has you written all over it. Your greed. Your shrewdness. My guess is Gorman here approached you first. And you sold Roscoe on it. But that's only a guess."

She said, "It's a bad guess, Mal. I had nothing to do with this hoax. If indeed it is a hoax. . . ."

"It's a hoax. I can prove it. And I'm going to prove it before your precious book comes out."

Gorman stood; cleared his throat, smiled patronizingly. Laughed: heh-heh-heh. Said: "Look, Mallory. Let's explore some possibilities. First, I'm protected on this thing. If you want to get my ass in a jam, you're not gonna."

"How do you figure that?"

"Let's keep this hypothetical. Let's hypothetically say I talked Roscoe Kane into hypothetically faking this Hammett book."

"Yeah. Let's hypothetically say that."

"Suppose I hypothetically set things up so it looks like I'm an innocent party."

"How could you have done that?"

He smiled and shrugged.

And then Mae came clean.

She walked up to me, looked right at me, so close I could smell her; she smelled good—jasmine, soap or perfume, I don't know what. But jasmine.

And she said, "Mal, it's true. Gregg's covered himself. He planted the manuscript among legitimate materials he acquired."

"From that rental library in California he bought out?"

"Yes. And the person who previously owned those materials was a publisher who Roscoe had done work

181

for; and that man, who Roscoe was linked to, died of natural causes two years ago. So if this should all . . . come to light, Gregg Gorman will come out unblemished."

"But minus six figures from Random House," I said.

"A good share of that money went to Roscoe," Mae said, "so you'd be taking it from me, Mal. And at what expense?"

"What do you mean?"

"You'd be tarnishing Roscoe's name; you'd brand him forever in the public consciousness as a fraud. A criminal, even. Can you do that to my husband's memory?"

"As someone once said, Mae—you're good. You're very good."

"Please, Mal."

"Please what?"

"Please think of Roscoe. It . . . was weak of me, of him, to get involved in this. But you know what his situation was; you know he couldn't publish anything in this country, hadn't published anything in years. It was a second chance for us. And Gregg was going to publish Roscoe's own books, and . . . it was a new start."

"Only it made him depressed."

Sadness fell across her face like a veil. "Yes. He began to drink. Heavily. You know that."

"He lost his self-respect," I said, "getting involved in this scam. Didn't you know that would happen?"

She laughed. Bitter little laugh. "He didn't have any self-respect left. Not until he finished writing Hammett's book. . . ."

"And reminded himself how good he was."

She laughed again. Sardonic little laugh. "That's right. *The Secret Emperor* gave him his self-respect back. . . ."

"And took it away, at the same time."

Mae sighed. "I loved him, Mal. I didn't mean for it to go this way."

"What way?"

"For him to . . . drink himself to death."

"Oh. You mean get drunk and drown himself in the tub. Accidentally."

"Or whatever. It was suicide, in a way."

"You were convinced it was murder, yesterday."

"I . . . I don't think it was. I've been thinking. Having second thoughts. I just don't think those wet towels mean anything. We were clutching at straws. . . ."

"Or damp towels."

Firmly, resolutely, she said, "I think we were wrong, Mal. I think Roscoe just . . . died. Hard to accept, I know. Probably hard for you to accept your hero being involved in a . . . scam, as you call this. But he was. He was. Life doesn't work out like it does in books . . . does it, Mal?"

"Rarely," I said.

"Do you think less of Roscoe, for what he did?"

"No."

"Do you . . . think less of me?"

"Mae," I said, "I hardly think of you at all."

Tears ran down her cheeks. She bit her lip and turned and went into the bathroom and sat on the stool and wept.

Suddenly Gorman's hand was on my shoulder. The last time he did that, I punched him in the stomach.

This time I just turned and looked into his grinning face; it gave me a much closer look at that food-flecked goatee and those yellow teeth than I ever hoped to have. The beady buglike eyes were moving back and forth. He was smiling. He'd had a revelation.

"How'd you like a piece of the action?" he said.

I smiled and shook my head. Unbelievable.

"How 'bout some action?" he went on. "Then you can keep your idol's name clean and make a few bucks on the deal, to boot. Why not. Let's say ten grand now, and and another ten six months after the book's published—assuming everything's goin' as planned."

"Is this hypothetical?"

"Yeah, sure. You want ten hypothetical grand or not?"

I looked at his nervous, grinning countenance, and then at Mae, sitting on the stool in the bathroom looking up now, tear-streaked face otherwise blank, but the eyes were appraising me. Kathy was standing by the door; frozen.

"I'll think about it," I said.

"Good," Gorman said.

"Good," Mae said, smiling bravely.

"The awards ceremony is at two," I said to her. "Don't forget."

She nodded. "I won't forget."

I turned back to Gorman. "You going to be there?"

"Sure," he said. "I'm a speaker."

"Oh, really?"

"Yeah. PWA asked me to say a few words about this important Hammett book we discovered." And he smiled at me buddy-buddy and put his hand on my shoulder.

"Don't do that," I said. "Even if I take your ten grand, don't do that."

His smile disappeared and he backed off. "You got no soul, Mallory. No heart and soul."

"I had 'em removed in childhood," I said, "along with my scruples."

From the bathroom, Mae in a monotone said, "Gat Garson. Chapter Four, *Trouble Wears a Skirt*."

"Correct, Mae," I nodded to her, and took Kathy by the arm and got the hell out of there.

17

WE went to the Artistic Café for lunch, again, and
Kathy questioned me about *The Secret Emperor.* I told
her the novel's plot was pretty much as indicated in
the 5000-word fragment Hammett had left of it.

The action begins in San Francisco but quickly
moves to Washington, D.C., and Baltimore. Hammett's nameless detective, the Continental Op, is sent
east to trace a stolen document, a seemingly nondes-
cript assignment. In the course of the case he soon
becomes involved with the exotic daughter of mil-
lionaire Sheth Gutman. Gutman, frustrated that he
can never hope to run for the presidency because he's
a Jew, plans to become "secret emperor of the United
States," by getting his own man, a crooked senator,
elected president. The Op is drawn into a labyrinth
of corruption on high levels—in political, military
and industrial circles. The finale, a paraphrase of a
Hammett short story, "The Gutting of Couffignal,"
and a foreshadowing of the conclusion of *The Maltese
Falcon,* has the Op rejecting the advances of Gutman's
daughter, who has betrayed him, and turning her
over to Secret Service agents.

"In short," I told her over cheeseburgers, "it's the
best novel Hammett never wrote."

"Was the Gutman name in Hammett's fragment?" she asked. "Or was that an embellishment of Roscoe Kane's?" Gutman, of course, was also the name of the famous, villainous "fat man" of *The Maltese Falcon.*

"That was in Hammett's fragment," I said. "I've never read the fragment, incidentally, but it's been summarized in articles and in various Hammett biographies—including Cynthia Crystal's. As I recall, the detective hero of Hammett's version *wasn't* the Op, though. That, apparently, was a Roscoe Kane embellishment."

"I wonder why he did that?"

I swallowed a bite of cheeseburger, sipped some Coke through a straw and answered. "Actually, it's one of the tip-offs that the book's a fake. Hammett had begun the book with a different protagonist, a hero who doesn't appear in any of his other stories or novels. But since the fragment was only five thousand words, there wasn't much for another writer to pick up on and run with, where the character was concerned. Better to treat the fragment as a false start, and rework it, substituting an established Hammett hero."

She nodded, seeing it. "The Op's the hero of dozens of short stories and several novels. That gave Kane a lot to draw from. Gave him a frame of reference."

"Right. And don't forget, Roscoe was a real Hammett fancier. He was intimate with the Op tales. Knew 'em by heart."

"Why were you so suspicious, Mal, even before you read the manuscript?"

"Well, Gorman's involvement, on principle. But keep in mind that Gorman's a publisher himself—as if I had to remind you; he'll plead that he felt Mystery House was too small to properly publish the Hammett book, hence the need to sell it off to a major publisher. Which is twaddle. A book like that would've *made* Mystery House a major publisher. Gorman was after a quick financial kill. Also, the fact that the Hammett estate is getting 'a piece of the action,' as Gorman puts it, made me wary."

"Surely you don't mean to imply the estate's involved in the hoax. . . ."

"No! They're its victims, like everybody else. But Gorman had hold of an unpublished manuscript by a dead author, for which he owned certain publishing rights outright. Now, if my rudimentary understanding of copyright is correct, Gorman could've copyrighted that work himself and left the Hammett estate out in the cold."

"What's the point of Gregg giving the estate a share when he could've had it all for himself?"

"That *is* the point. The estate getting a share in the proceeds legitimizes the book—and is an incentive for the estate to not question the 'experts' whose opinions authenticated the work—which is by any standards a brilliant forgery."

"But when you read it, you saw right through it."

"Sure."

"What element of the plot was it that you recognized?"

"Huh?"

"You told Mae and Gorman you recognized elements from that unpublished novel of Kane's."

"Oh, that. That was a lie."

She dropped her sandwich and her jaw. "A *lie?*"

"Sure. Roscoe never gave me an unpublished book of his. He had a rule: if it's bad, burn it. He didn't leave any false starts or unsuccessful manuscripts behind, believe me."

"But . . . that was how you were going to *prove* the Hammett book was a fake . . . that was your *evidence.* . . ."

"Yeah, well, I was bluffing."

She looked at me like a child at the zoo seeing a monkey for the first time.

"You were *bluffing?*" she said, incredulous.

"That's right. I recognized signs of Roscoe in that book, sure. Plenty of 'em. But subtle ones. I could make a very convincing case for it being ghosted by Roscoe, yes, but there would be no dramatic, obvious revelations. It'd be almost a scholarly piece of work."

"But, then . . . you don't have anything . . . nothing you can go to the authorities or the media with. . . ."

"Sure I do. Mae and Gorman admitted their scam in front of witnesses."

"Who?"

"You and me. Us. Remember?"

"Oh." She looked at her cheeseburger blankly. "Right." She looked at me blankly. "Got any other surprises for me?"

"Sure. I'm going to accept Gorman's ten-grand bribe."

"What?"

"Once I have his check in my hands, I *will* have some solid evidence of a scam."

She shook her head. "I didn't really begin to see this coming. You fooled me completely. I really thought there was an unpublished book by Roscoe Kane."

I grinned at her. "There's a lot of that going around. Plenty of people are believing there's an unpublished Hammett book, too."

She shot a smirky grin back at me. "It's nice of you to clear all this with me, before involving me. As a witness and all."

I reached across and touched her hand; wiped the smug smile off my face. "Kathy, it couldn't be helped. I had no idea Gorman was going to be in Mae's room. It was all impromptu. I'm an old Second City fan, remember? And this is Chicago. Improv comedy and fiction-writing are the same animal; like they say, you come up with 'something wonderful, right away.'"

Wry smile #732. "You're a lunatic."

"Yeah. But nice, as lunatics go."

"So much for me editing *Noir*."

"When I'm through with Gorman, the only publication he'll be involved with is the prison newspaper."

She managed to eat most of her cheeseburger and pretty soon we were walking back to the Americana-Congress, hand in hand. Another gloomy day, but I felt good. Then my stomach fell: just as we were approaching the front entrance of the hotel, G. Roger Donaldson came out, in his lime-color blazer and reddish blond beard.

His eyes narrowing in on me, he moved toward me like a small car.

"I had hoped to run into you, Mr. Mallory," he said, parking in front of me, folding his thick arms, eyes hard and green and angry.

"That doesn't surprise me," I admitted.

Kathy moved away from me. Deserting the sinking ship.

"There's something you should've known about me," he said, unfolding his arms, smiling, not in a least bit friendly way. "I will abide no man's insolence without a due and dispassionate revenge. . . ."

"Does that mean you're going to hit me now?"

"Fuckin' A," he said, and decked me.

I picked myself up, Kathy looked on wide-eyed and open-mouthed, and he was just about to haul off again when I held out two hands in a conciliatory gesture.

"Truce," I said, licking blood out of the corner of my mouth. "Give me a minute!"

He stopped in midswing and appraised the situation.

Kathy looked at me, wondering what I was going to do.

The hotel doorman, observing all this from a few yards away, was wondering whether or not to summon a cop.

I was wondering how to express what I felt. Donaldson doing a macho number on me made me realize how ridiculous I had been behaving lately: defending myself and Kathy in that alley had been one thing; the rest of my behavior was another—verbally attacking Gorman in the dealers' room, then punching him in the stomach in the bar, finally humiliating Donaldson on that panel and stalking off.

"I deserved that," I said. "I was a jerk this morning. And you deserve an apology. I want to give you one, now, privately—and I plan to give you one publicly. That's a promise."

He eyed me suspiciously; Kathy had a disapproving expression, as if I'd suddenly turned coward.

Which wasn't true, but what would've been so bad if I had? I'm not Gat Garson; nobody is. I couldn't go around behaving like a macho jerk and not have it catch up with me. Maybe it was going to catch up with me now, in the form of a severe beating from this apparently very fit—and fit to be tied—would-be Hemingway.

"You're just trying to weasel out of it," Donaldson said.

"No," I said. "I'm a little afraid of you, sure, but I really don't like you, so the jackass in me would relish trading some punches with you. I'm just trying to get the jackass in me in harness, okay?"

191

He smiled, just a little. And suddenly seemed sort of embarrassed himself. "Okay," he said. "I think I get your point. Maybe I ought to keep my own jackass in harness. But I'm going to hold you to that public apology."

"You deserve that much. Mind you, I stand behind what I said on that panel. You ought to apologize to the ghosts of Hammett and Chandler, in public, but that's up to you and your conscience. My conscience says I was rude to one of my fellow writers, and in public, and shame on me."

I held out my hand and Donaldson first shook his head and then the hand.

"Can two men who don't like each other be friends?" he asked, smiling.

"I doubt it," I said. "I'm not into male bonding. But I'm going to do you a favor. At least I will, if you'll do me one."

Donaldson tilted his head, looked at me suspiciously again. "Oh? What favor are you going to do me?"

"I'm going to save you from some heavy duty embarrassment. . . ."

And Kathy, Donaldson and I went into the hotel and up to my room for a little talk.

18

By one-thirty the Gold Room was full; most everyone at the convention was there. So were various representatives of the press, including TV news teams, minicams and all, here from channels 7 and 9, the rival groups at either side of the stage. The table where I'd sat earlier today, on the panel, was still strewn with microphones and water glasses, but there was also a podium at the center now, behind which a smiling and a little bit nervous Tom Sardini was assembling some note cards and the award plaques and other material. As the current president of the Private Eye Writers of America, Tom was to be master of ceremonies.

The room was buzzing, but people were keeping their voices down—perhaps out of respect for the late Roscoe Kane. It was no secret Roscoe was this year's recipient of the Life Achievement Award; though technically under wraps, it had been leaked by Tom to the media, and naturally the word had then traveled around the convention as well. The five hundred or more people in the room all whispering created a cloud of noise that hung over the room, as if threatening a storm.

I was sitting with Kathy in the front row; Donaldson was seated next to her. Just behind Donaldson was Gregg Gorman, looking as spiffy as he could manage, in a tweedy sports coat with patched elbows, a brown knit tie and a more or less clean tan shirt. Sardini had asked him to "say a few words" about the Hammett book, at the close of the ceremony. Next to him was Mae Kane. She still wore the clingy black dress with black gloves and a pearl necklace; she looked a little like a blond Morticia Addams.

Donaldson leaned back and whispered to Gorman; Gorman listened, eyes wide, then glanced at me, eyes slitted, and I nodded at him. Gorman smiled broadly and nodded and reached in his coat pocket and took out a checkbook. He made out a check, handed it to Donaldson and Donaldson, with a sage little nod, handed it over to me.

The check, on the Mystery House account, was for ten thousand dollars. At lower left a notation: editorial services, *Secret Emperor.*

I glanced back at Gorman and he was still smiling broadly, one pal to another; he nodded at me and I nodded back, but couldn't manage to summon a smile, even a fake one. Mae Kane looked at me warily. I was able to find a little reassuring smile for her, but she didn't seem to buy it. Smart woman.

Glancing back around, I noticed, on the other side of the room, Jerome Kane, seated quietly in an aisle seat, gazing back at me with his father's china-blue eyes. His attire was stylishly somber, black jacket and gray slacks and gray tie; his friend Troy apparently was not with him—the rest of his row was taken up by a preoccupied-looking Tim Culver, sitting next to Cynthia Crystal, who was sitting next to four women of varying ages who were talking with (actually, at) Cynthia, drawing-room mystery fans no doubt. They were in the right place, then: the Gold Room was one big drawing room today. . . .

By now it was standing room only, but a few people were lining the walls; at my right, one of those people was an orange-haired woman in a green dress with a brown purse on a strap over her shoulder.

Evelyn Kane.

She looked nice today. She'd had her hair done, and the green dress had a sheen to it, looked new, and fit her matronly figure nicely. She had a corsage on, as well. She looked like a chaperone at a senior prom.

My eyes caught hers.

A nasty little smile settled in one side of her mouth; she nodded. I nodded back, wondering what the smile meant.

As inconspicuously as possible, I pointed Jerome and Evelyn out to Kathy.

"Just like Charlie Chan," I said to her, *sotto voce.*

"What?"

"All the suspects are gathered."

"What're you talking about?"

"Jerome, Evelyn, Gorman, or Mae. Or a combination thereof. Killed Roscoe Kane, I mean."

Kathy looked at me like a mother at her bonehead child. "Gorman couldn't have done it, Mal. He had an alibi, remember?"

"Sure. He said he was eating with his angels, at the Berghoff. Only I called the Berghoff, and they close at ten. Even if he and his friends lingered well past closing, his alibi's shot. Roscoe was drowned some time between eleven and midnight, remember."

That would've sobered her, if she hadn't been sober already.

Tom, up on the stage, motioned at me.

195

"Save my place," I told Kathy, and went up and joined him.

"This is great, Mal," he said. "Do you see how many *people* are here? All this media? The PWA couldn't *pay* for this kind of publicity."

"That's true," I said.

"Well, I just want you to know I appreciate your making sure Mae Kane was here. Without her, we don't have much of a show."

"That's also true," I said. "But don't thank me yet. You better see how this goes. . . ."

"I'm sure it'll be smooth as glass. Are you excited, Mal?"

"Uh, sure. About what?"

"Don't give me that. About being up for best hard-cover, you dope! You got an acceptance speech ready?"

I won't claim I'd forgotten about being nominated, but it hadn't been the foremost thing in my mind today.

I said, "You don't have an inside track, do you? 'Cause I don't have anything prepared. . . ."

Tom shook his head no. "I don't know who the winners are. The results were given to me in sealed envelopes by the awards chairman; and the plaques are sealed up, too. But I think you've got a chance, Mal. I like your book."

"It probably shouldn't even've been nominated; the hero isn't technically a private eye. Aren't you up for something?"

"Yeah," he admitted. "Best softcover."

"Luck to you," I said.

"Thanks, Mal. Thanks for everything."

At two the awards ceremony started; R. Edward Porter, as one of the most respected short-story writers in the field, presented the short-story award to former

196

Ellery Queen Mystery Magazine critic Jon Breen, who gave a brief self-effacing speech and sat down. Then best softcover was presented by last year's winner, William Campbell Gault, who upon opening the envelope said, "Ah—the fix is in, I see."

Tom had won, for his latest Jacob Miles novel; red-faced, he apologized for winning the award—then admitted he had helped found the organization in hopes that one day this might happen. That got a good, sincere laugh from the crowd, who applauded his honesty; the applause turned into a standing ovation and Tom just stood there, award in hand—a fancy wood plaque on which the cover of his book was embossed—and grinned like a kid on Christmas morning.

I looked past Kathy down at Donaldson and said, "Good luck."

He was up for best hardcover, too; for *Poisonous Wine.*

He said, "And to you."

We both lost; Bill DeAngelo won, for his latest Mark Kaub book. Bill said that since he hadn't won an Edgar lately, he was very pleased to receive this. His delivery was funny, and he seemed genuinely grateful, and returned to his seat before the applause had died down.

Then Tom took the podium again and said, "We've saved the most important award for last—the Life Achievement Award. I suppose it's no surprise to anyone here that this year's award goes to Roscoe Kane. The loss of this important author, on the eve of receiving this recognition, is a tragic one. I've asked a good friend—and student—of Roscoe Kane's, to say a few words, and introduce Mrs. Kane . . . who will receive the award for her husband. Mal?"

And I got up from the audience and climbed onto the stage and stood behind the podium. The minicams were trained on me. So was the crowd's full attention.

"Roscoe Kane wasn't a perfect man," I said into the microphone; my voice was loud enough to do without a mike, so using one made it boom through the room, giving my words a certain added weight—and ominousness. "Roscoe Kane wasn't even a perfect writer. His gift was a narrow one. Yet he was a genius of sorts. Like Edgar Rice Burroughs was a genius of sorts; or Ian Fleming; or Mickey Spillane. He created a vivid character in Gat Garson—like Tarzan and James Bond and Mike Hammer—a larger-than-life hero who, I think, will live on for as long as people like to read a good yarn. Which I trust will be forever.

"But Roscoe Kane wasn't larger than life. I think his work may prove to be larger than death, but never mind. Roscoe was a flawed, eccentric man, and I loved him like a father."

Halfway back in the audience, stage right, Jerome Kane leaned forward in his seat.

My voice continued to rumble through the big room: "I have to reveal something, now, that—unfortunately—may cast a shadow on Roscoe Kane's reputation."

Gregg Gorman leaned forward in his seat; Mae Kane covered her eyes with a gloved hand.

"You are all aware, I'm sure, of the forthcoming 'recently discovered' Dashiell Hammett novel, *The Secret Emperor* . . . only, the *novel* wasn't 'discovered.' It was concoted out of a five thousand word fragment by Hammett, whose authenticity is not in any doubt. The novel, which is based on that genuine fragment, was written by Roscoe Kane."

A collective gasp went up.

The reporters and TV people, at stage left and right, seemed to wake up; eyes popped open.

And Gregg Gorman, sitting forward in his seat, looked at me with red-faced anger.

"Roscoe Kane was a bitter man," I said. "He had been blacklisted, or so he felt, by the publishing community; no new Gat Garson novels had been published in this country in fifteen years. He had also been largely ignored by mystery fiction's fan community, their critics and reviewers. In his heart, Roscoe knew he was a mystery writer of the first rank; and when he was given the opportunity to finish a novel by *his* hero, Dashiell Hammett, he jumped at the chance. To prove his worth. And to put one over on those who'd blacklisted and rejected him. The publishers. The fans."

The room got very quiet. Gorman had sat back in his chair, but his face was still very red. Jerome Kane had a small smile; Evelyn Kane did, too. In the front row, Kathy looked a little frightened. And Mae Kane was crying quietly into a handkerchief.

"The first person to cast doubt on the authenticity of *The Secret Emperor* was G. Roger Donaldson," I said. "Mr. Donaldson—who on this very stage received some rude treatment from me this morning, for which I apologize—came to me with his suspicions. He'd read the manuscript, having been asked by its 'discoverer' to help verify its authorship; at first he'd been convinced. But then he had second thoughts. It occurred to him that Roscoe Kane might have been capable of having written this and, after Kane's suspicious drowning, Donaldson approached me with a copy of the manuscript. He wanted my opinion as a Roscoe Kane authority. Did I think Kane might have ghosted this book?"

199

Donaldson, next to Kathy, smiling faintly, nodded at me.

I went on: "I read *The Secret Emperor* last night. Through internal evidence, I can prove Kane wrote this book. His literary fingerprints are all over it. But I would like to add that it *is* a first-rate Hammett pastiche. I would trust it *will* one day see print, and enhance Roscoe Kane's reputation—at least his literary reputation.

"Now, as to the question of who is responsible for this hoax—who has attempted to swindle Random House and all of you mystery fans out of your money— it is of course none other than my good, good friend Gregg Gorman. . . ."

Gorman stood and thrust a finger toward me. "That's a lie!" Without a microphone, his voice had a hollow, impotent quality, about as forceful as a stone rattling around in a can.

But he shouted on: "A complete fabrication! You have no proof, Mallory! Get him off the stage, some-body—aren't there any security guards in this joint?"

I took the check out of my pocket. My voice coming out of the loudspeakers was like the voice of God, where Gorman was concerned. "When I confronted Gregg Gorman earlier today, he offered me ten thou-sand dollars, up front, to keep quiet about Kane's ghost job; and ten thousand more, six months after the book's publication. He made this offer in front of a witness. He gave me this check in front of several more. G. Roger Donaldson and Kathy Wickman, specifically."

Donaldson and Kathy stood and turned toward the audience and nodded their heads.

Then they sat down.

So did Gorman, defeated; sat down heavily and slumped forward. He looked, as if for help, toward Mae Kane. Mae Kane didn't look at him.

I continued. "I hope you people, and the thousands upon thousands of mystery readers you represent, will not look too unkindly on Roscoe Kane. He paid a heavy price for his involvement in this fraud; much heavier than the loss of his reputation. Roscoe Kane was my hero—but he was also a man. A flawed one—as has been every man I've ever met, to one degree or another. But I do think he had in mind to do something—something that, had he been able to do it, would've made him look better, in your eyes, and posterity's."

The room was dead silent; five-hundred-some rapt faces were fixed on me . . . everyone in the room was looking at me—except Gorman and Mae Kane, the former gazing downward, the latter staring blankly off to her left, her tears dried, now.

"I believe Roscoe Kane intended to reveal his authorship of the so-called Hammett book," I said. I spoke softly, but it came across loud—not so much because of the loudspeakers, but because of the words themselves. "I believe he intended to reveal this all along. But initially, I think, he planned to allow the book to be published, and be received well by the critics and readers; then, possibly, he planned to pack up his share of the loot and head for Mexico or somewhere. But I know . . . knew . . . Roscoe. I know his ego. He would've told. Eventually he would've told. He'd have wanted his horse laugh on the publishing industry. He'd have wanted to have the last word with the fans. And his killer knew that."

The room got noisy, then, but quieted down when I continued: "Yes—his killer. Because Roscoe Kane was murdered. I discovered his body, with his wife Mae. The evidence on the scene indicated murder, but the Chicago coroner's office disregarded it, and my theories. So, today, in public, in front of this audience and these television cameras, I challenge the city of Chicago to reopen the death of Roscoe Kane, for a possible—probable—homicide investigation."

The room went beserk; murmuring escalated into near shouting, and the TV minicam cameramen bore down on me, and reporters with microphones were moving in, too.

"Please," I said, motioning to them to keep back. "Allow me to continue. I believe Roscoe had decided to reveal his complicity in the Hammett hoax, *before* publication of the book. And because of that, I think he was murdered. I think the murder was impromptu, almost a crime of passion, motivated though it was primarily by greed. And I also think I know who did it."

A hush fell over the room; I looked at Evelyn Kane— she looked at me.

"I know who did it, and I'm prepared to share my opinion and my reasons for it with the police. Unfortunately, it would not be proper for me to share it with you people, here."

The room got noisy again, and I had to call out to be heard, even with the microphone: "Right now, there's an award to be presented—to Mae Kane, Mrs. Roscoe Kane, would you please step forward?"

The room got funeral-parlor quiet again, and Mae rose from the audience like an apparition in black. She floated to the front of the room, the silver arcs of her hair swinging gently, and took the plaque from me. The plaque pictured the cover of *Kill Me, Darling*, the first Gat Garson novel; she didn't look at it, though. She looked at me. Her face was white; her expression was blank; the tracks of tears could be seen against her pale makeup.

"Mal," she said. "Why did you do this?"

I leaned across the table and pretended to be looking at the plaque, smiling as I did. The room was noisy again, people discussing, arguing, the revelations I'd dropped in their laps; the media people were keeping their distance from me at the moment.

I was away from the microphone now; no one could hear me but Mae.

I whispered: "You did it, Mae. You did it. Roscoe and Evelyn were getting back together. Her companionship offered him more than your bed ever could. She gave him his self-respect back; she'd convinced him to expose you and Gorman and the whole scheme, before the fact. So that he'd be the hero of the piece, the media star. So that his career might be able to start all over again, and you'd be left behind."

She looked at me with wide, empty eyes.

I said, "When the police investigate, they'll find it all out, easy enough. You arrived at the hotel and went up to his room—you knew what name he'd registered under. Did you ask for a key at the desk, or was the room unlocked? No matter. You went in and took off your coat and drowned him; then you put your coat back on over your clothes and disposed of the wet towels you'd sopped the bathroom floor up with, and you came down to the lounge and found me. And made a fall guy out of me, as Gat Garson would say. I found it a little odd that you left your coat on after we found Roscoe, even when you lay down on the bed, but I didn't make much of it; then it occurred to me you might've left it on because your clothes under there were wet, still wet. From drowning him."

203

The wide eyes filled with tears; actress tears? I couldn't tell.

Then, softly, so that no one could hear but me, she answered: "I didn't plan it. He was asleep in the tub. I held him under; he didn't even wake up. He didn't suffer. He just went away. . . ."

The sounds of the shots shattered all else—stopped all discussion in the room; two shots, loud startling, commanding all attention.

Mae Kane's wide eyes went wider still, as the impact threw her forward; then like a ragdoll she flopped back, keeping on her feet somehow, Raggedy Ann managing to stand impossibly up, and she looked down at her black dress. Two red holes, stacked one atop the other, like two periods ending sentences, like a bright red colon: then blood welled out the bottom one, turning it into a semicolon; she covered the semicolon with both hands and then brought them away from her, looked at them, the blood on them, and tried to scream.

But didn't make it.

She fell forward, against the table, knocking the podium off, her bloody hand touching my shirt as I leaned forward toward her. I looked up.

Evelyn Kane was standing in the aisle behind where Mae Kane had stood; smiling like a skull. Holding a long-barreled .38 in her two gripped hands, the proper firing stance Roscoe had taught her when he'd schooled her in the use of a Garson gat such as this. The flap of the brown purse slung over her shoulder was open from where she'd withdrawn the revolver. Slowly she lowered the still smoking gun and let go of it; let it drop. It clunked on the floor near Mae.

People were standing and shouting, a few screaming, a few even scurrying out of the room.

But it had happened so fast, most of them were just standing there, like me. The two bullets had cut